Different men will find different ways of praising life, of calling it good.

Even I, who by my nature cannot fight or destroy, can see intellectually this truth: In a war against death, it is by fighting and destroying the enemy that the value of life is affirmed.

In such a war, no living fighter need concern himself with pity for his enemy; this one twisted pain, at least, no one need feel.

But in any war the vital effect of pacifism is not on the foe, but on the pacifist.

I touched a peace-loving mind, very hungry for life . . .

BERSERKER

FRED SABERHAGEN

ACE SCIENCE FICTION BOOKS
NEW YORK

BERSERKER

An Ace Science Fiction Book / published by arrangement with
the author

PRINTING HISTORY
Tenth printing / April 1984

ISBN: 0-441-05480-3

Ace Science Fiction Books are published by The Berkley Publishing Group,
200 Madison Avenue, New York, New York 10016.
PRINTED IN THE UNITED STATES OF AMERICA

INTRODUCTION

I, THIRD HISTORIAN OF THE CARMPAN RACE, in gratitude to the Earth-descended race for their defense of my world, set down here for them my fragmentary vision of their great war against our common enemy.

The vision has been formed piece by piece through my contacts in past and present time with the minds of men and of machines. In these minds alien to me I often perceive what I cannot understand, yet what I see is true. And so I have truly set down the acts and words of Earth-descended men great and small and ordinary, the words and even the secret thoughts of your heroes and your traitors.

Looking into the past I have seen how in the twentieth century of your Christian calendar your forefathers on Earth first built radio detectors capable of sounding the deeps of interstellar space. On the day when whispers in our alien voices were first detected, straying in across the enormous intervals, the universe of stars became real to all Earth's nations and all her tribes.

They became aware of the real world surrounding them—a universe strange and immense beyond thought, possibly hostile, surrounding and shrinking all Earthmen alike. Like island savages just become aware of the great powers existing on and beyond their ocean, your nations began—sullenly, mistrustfully, almost against their will—to put aside their quarrels with one another.

In the same century the men of old Earth took their first steps into space. They studied our alien voices whenever they could hear us. And when the men of old Earth began to travel faster than light, they followed our voices to seek us out.

Your race and mine studied each other with eager science and with great caution and courtesy. We Carmpan and our older friends are more passive than you. We live in different environments and think mainly in different directions. We posed no threat to Earth. We saw to it that Earthmen were not crowded by our presence; physically and mentally they had to stretch to touch us. Ours, all the skills of keeping peace. Alas, for the day unthinkable that was to come, the day when we wished ourselves warlike!

You of Earth found uninhabited planets, where you could thrive in the warmth of suns much like your own. In large colonies and small you scattered yourselves across one segment of one arm of our slow-turning galaxy. To your settlers and frontiersmen the galaxy began to seem a friendly place, rich in worlds hanging ripe for your peaceful occupation.

The alien immensity surrounding you appeared to be not hostile after all. Imagined threats had receded behind horizons of silence and vastness. And so once more you allowed among yourselves the luxury of dangerous conflict, carrying the threat of suicidal violence.

No enforceable law existed among the planets. On each of your scattered colonies individual leaders maneuvered for personal power, distracting their people with real or imagined dangers posed by other Earth-descended men.

All further exploration was delayed, in the very days when the new and inexplicable radio voices were first heard drifting in from beyond your frontiers, the strange soon-to-be-terrible voices that conversed only in mathematics. Earth and Earth's colonies were divided each against all by suspicion, and in mutual fear were rapidly training and arming for war.

And at this point the very readiness for violence that had sometimes so nearly destroyed you, proved to be the means of life's survival. To us, the Carmpan watchers, the withdrawn seers and touchers of minds, it appeared that you had carried the crushing weight of war through all your history knowing that it would at last be needed, that this hour would strike when nothing less awful would serve.

When the hour struck and our enemy came without warning, you were ready with swarming battle-fleets. You were dispersed and dug in on scores of planets, and heavily armed. Because you were, some of you and some of us are now alive.

Not all our Carmpan psychology, our logic and vision and subtlety, would have availed us anything. The skills of peace and tolerance were useless, for our enemy was not alive.

What is thought, that mechanism seems to bring it forth?

WITHOUT A THOUGHT

THE MACHINE WAS a vast fortress, containing no life, set by its long-dead masters to destroy anything that lived. It and many others like it were the inheritance of Earth from some war fought between unknown interstellar empires, in some time that could hardly be connected with any Earthly calendar.

One such machine could hang over a planet colonized by men and in two days pound the surface into a lifeless cloud of dust and steam, a hundred miles deep. This particular machine had already done just that.

It used no predictable tactics in its dedicated, unconscious war against life. The ancient, unknown gamesmen had built it as a random factor, to be loosed in the enemy's territory to do what damage it might. Men thought its plan of battle was chosen by the random disintegrations of atoms in a block of some long-lived isotope buried deep inside it, and so was not even in theory predictable by opposing brains, human or electronic.

Men called it a berserker.

Del Murray, sometime computer specialist, had called it other names than that; but right now he was too busy to waste breath, as he moved in staggering lunges around the little cabin of his one-man fighter, plugging in replacement units for equipment damaged by the last near-miss of a berserker missile. An animal resembling a large dog with an ape's forelegs moved around the cabin too, carrying in its nearly human hands a supply of emergency sealing patches. The cabin air was full of haze. Wherever movement of the haze showed a leak to an unpressurized part of the hull, the dog-ape moved to apply a patch.

"Hello, Foxglove!" the man shouted, hoping that his radio was again in working order.

"Hello, Murray, this is Foxglove," said a sudden loud voice in the cabin. "How far did you get?"

Del was too weary to show much relief that his communications were open again. "I'll let you know in a minute. At least it's stopped shooting at me for a while. Move, Newton." The alien animal, pet and ally, called an *aiyan*, moved away from the man's feet and kept singlemindedly looking for leaks.

After another minute's work Del could strap his body into the deep-cushioned command chair again, with something like an operational panel before him. That last near-miss had sprayed the whole cabin with fine penetrating splinters. It was remarkable that man and *aiyan* had come through unwounded.

2

His radar working again, Del could say: "I'm about ninety miles out from it, Foxglove. On the opposite side from you." His present position was the one he had been trying to achieve since the battle had begun.

The two Earth ships and the berserker were half a light year from the nearest sun. The berserker could not leap out of normal space, toward the defenseless colonies of the planets of that sun, while the two ships stayed close to it. There were only two men aboard Foxglove. They had more machinery working for them than did Del, but both manned ships were mites compared to their opponent.

Del's radar showed him an ancient ruin of metal, not much smaller in cross section than New Jersey. Men had blown holes in it the size of Manhattan Island, and melted puddles of slag as big as lakes upon its surface.

But the berserker's power was still enormous. So far no man had fought it and survived. Now, it could squash Del's little ship like a mosquito; it was wasting its unpredictable subtlety on him. Yet there was a special taste of terror in the very difference of it. Men could never frighten this enemy, as it frightened them.

Earthmen's tactics, worked out from bitter experience against other berserkers, called for a simultaneous attack by three ships. Foxglove and Murray made two. A third was supposedly on the way, but still about eight hours distant, moving at C-plus velocity, outside of normal space. Until it arrived, Foxglove and Murray must hold the berserker at bay, while it brooded unguessable schemes.

It might attack either ship at any moment, or it might seek to disengage. It might wait hours for them to make the first move—though it would certainly fight if the

3

men attacked it. It had learned the language of Earth's spacemen—it might try to talk with them. But always, ultimately, it would seek to destroy them and every other living thing it met. That was the basic command given it by the ancient warlords.

A thousand years ago, it would easily have swept ships of the type that now opposed it from its path, whether they carried fusion missiles or not. Now, it was in some electrical way conscious of its own weakening by accumulated damage. And perhaps in long centuries of fighting its way across the galaxy it had learned to be wary.

Now, quite suddenly, Del's detectors showed force fields forming in behind his ship. Like the encircling arms of a huge bear they blocked his path away from the enemy. He waited for some deadly blow, with his hand trembling over the red button that would salvo his atomic missiles at the berserker—but if he attacked alone, or even with Foxglove, the infernal machine would parry their missiles, crush their ships, and go on to destroy another helpless planet. Three ships were needed to attack. The red firing button was now only a last desperate resort.

Del was reporting the force fields to Foxglove when he felt the first hint in his mind of another attack.

"Newton!" he called sharply, leaving the radio connection with Foxglove open. They would hear and understand what was going to happen.

The *aiyan* bounded instantly from its combat couch to stand before Del as if hypnotized, all attention riveted on the man. Del had sometimes bragged: "Show Newton a drawing of different-colored lights, convince

4

him it represents a particular control panel, and he'll push buttons or whatever you tell him, until the real panel matches the drawing.''

But no *aiyan* had the human ability to learn and to create on an abstract level; which was why Del was now going to put Newton in command of his ship.

He switched off the ship's computers—they were going to be as useless as his own brain under the attack he felt gathering—and said to Newton: "Situation Zombie.''

The animal responded instantly as it had been trained, seizing Del's hands with firm insistence and dragging them one at a time down beside the command chair to where the fetters had been installed.

Hard experience had taught men something about the berserkers' mind weapon, although its principles of operation were still unknown. It was slow in its onslaught, and its effects could not be steadily maintained for more than about two hours, after which a berserker was evidently forced to turn it off for an equal time. But while in effect, it robbed any human or electronic brain of the ability to plan or to predict—and left it unconscious of its own incapacity.

It seemed to Del that all this had happened before, maybe more than once. Newton, that funny fellow, had gone too far with his pranks; he had abandoned the little boxes of colored beads that were his favorite toys, and was moving the controls around at the lighted panel. Unwilling to share the fun with Del, he had tied the man to his chair somehow. Such behavior was really intolerable, especially when there was supposed to be a battle in progress. Del tried to pull his hands free, and called to Newton.

Newton whined earnestly, and stayed at the panel.

"Newt, you dog, come lemme loose. I know what I have to say: Four score and seven . . . hey, Newt, where're your toys? Lemme see your pretty beads." There were hundreds of tiny boxes of the varicolored beads, leftover trade goods that Newton loved to sort out and handle. Del peered around the cabin, chuckling a little at his own cleverness. He would get Newton distracted by the beads, and then . . . the vague idea faded into other crackbrained grotesqueries.

Newton whined now and then but stayed at the panel moving controls in the long sequence he had been taught, taking the ship through the feinting, evasive maneuvers that might fool a berserker into thinking it was still competently manned. Newton never put a hand near the big red button. Only if he felt deadly pain himself, or found a dead man in Del's chair, would he reach for that.

"Ah, roger, Murray," said the radio from time to time, as if acknowledging a message. Sometimes Foxglove added a few words or numbers that might have meant something. Del wondered what the talking was about.

At last he understood that Foxglove was trying to help maintain the illusion that there was still a competent brain in charge of Del's ship. The fear reaction came when he began to realize that he had once again lived through the effect of the mind weapon. The brooding berserker, half genius, half idiot, had forborne to press the attack when success would have been certain—perhaps deceived, perhaps following the strategy that avoided predictability at almost any cost.

"Newton." The animal turned, hearing a change in his voice. Now Del could say the words that would tell Newton it was safe to set his master free, a sequence too long for anyone under the mind weapon to recite.

"—shall not perish from the earth," he finished. With a yelp of joy Newton pulled the fetters from Del's hands. Del turned instantly to the radio.

"Effect has evidently been turned off, Foxglove," said Del's voice through the speaker in the cabin of the larger ship.

The Commander let out a sigh. "He's back in control!"

The Second Officer—there was no third—said: "That means we've got some kind of fighting chance, for the next two hours. I say let's attack now!"

The Commander shook his head, slowly but without hesitation. "With two ships, we don't have any real chance. Less than four hours until Gizmo gets here. We have to stall until then, if we want to win."

"It'll attack the next time it gets Del's mind scrambled! I don't think we fooled it for a minute . . . we're out of range of the mind beam here, but Del can't withdraw now. And we can't expect that *aiyan* to fight his ship for him. We'll really have no chance, with Del gone."

The Commander's eyes moved ceaselessly over his panel. We'll wait. We can't be sure it'll attack the next time it puts the beam on him . . ."

The berserker spoke suddenly, its radioed voice plain in the cabins of both ships: "I have a proposition for you, little ship." Its voice had a cracking, adolescent quality, because it strung together words and syllables recorded from the voices of human prisoners of both sexes and different ages. Bits of human emotion, sorted and fixed like butterflies on pins, thought the Commander. There was no reason to think it had kept the prisoners alive after learning the language from them.

"Well?" Del's voice sounded tough and capable by comparison.

"I have invented a game which we will play," it said. "If you play well enough, I will not kill you right away."

"Now I've heard everything," murmured the Second Officer.

After three thoughtful seconds the Commander slammed a fist on the arm of his chair. "It means to test his learning ability, to run a continuous check on his brain while it turns up the power of the mind beam and tries different modulations. If it can make sure the mind beam is working, it'll attack instantly. I'll bet my life on it. That's the game it's playing this time."

"I will think over your proposition," said Del's voice coolly.

The Commander said: "It's in no hurry to start. It won't be able to turn on the mind beam again for almost two hours."

"But we need another two hours beyond that."

Del's voice said: "Describe the game you want to play."

"It is a simplified version of the human game called checkers."

The Commander and the Second looked at each other, neither able to imagine Newton able to play checkers. Nor could they doubt that Newton's failure would kill them within a few hours, and leave another planet open to destruction.

After a minute's silence, Del's voice asked: "What'll we use for a board?"

"We will radio our moves to one another," said the berserker equably. It went on to describe a checkers-like game, played on a smaller board with less than the normal number of pieces. There was nothing very profound about it; but, of course, playing would seem to require a functional brain, human or electronic, able to plan and to predict.

"If I agree to play," said Del slowly, "how'll we decide who gets to move first?"

"He's trying to stall," said the Commander, gnawing a thumbnail. "We won't be able to offer any advice, with that thing listening. Oh, stay sharp, Del boy!"

"To simplify matters," said the berserker, "I will move first in every game."

Del could look forward to another hour free of the mind weapon when he finished rigging the checkerboard. When the pegged pieces were moved, appropriate signals would be radioed to the berserker; lighted squares on the board would show him where its pieces were moved. If it spoke to him while the mind weapon was on, Del's voice would answer from a tape, which he had stocked with vaguely aggressive phrases, such as: "Get on with the game," or "Do you want to give up now?"

He hadn't told the enemy how far along he was with his preparations because he was still busy with something the enemy must not know—the system that was going to enable Newton to play a game of simplified checkers.

Del gave a soundless little laugh as he worked, and glanced over to where Newton was lounging on his couch, clutching toys in his hands as if he drew some comfort from them. This scheme was going to push the *aiyan* near the limit of his ability, but Del saw no reason why it should fail.

Dell had completely analyzed the miniature checker

game, and diagrammed every position that Newton could possibly face—playing only even-numbered moves, thank the random berserker for that specification!—on small cards. Del had discarded some lines of play that would arise from some poor early moves by Newton, further simplifying his job. Now, on a card showing each possible remaining position, Del indicated the best possible move with a drawn-in arrow. Now he could quickly teach Newton to play the game by looking at the appropriate card and making the move shown by the arrow—

"Oh, oh," said Del, as his hands stopped working and he stared into space. Newton whined at the tone of his voice.

Once Del had sat at one board in a simultaneous chess exhibition, one of sixty players opposing the world champion, Blankenship. Del had held his own into the middle game. Then, when the great man paused again opposite his board, Del had shoved a pawn forward, thinking he had reached an unassailable position and could begin a counterattack. Blankenship had moved a rook to an innocent-looking square and strolled on to the next board—and then Del had seen the checkmate coming at him, four moves away but one move too late for him to do anything about it.

The Commander suddenly said a foul phrase in a loud distinct voice. Such conduct on his part was extremely rare, and the Second Officer looked round in surprise. "What?"

"I think we've had it." The Commander paused. "I hoped that Murray could set up some kind of a system over there, so that Newton could play the game—or appear to be playing it. But it won't work. Whatever system Newton plays by rote will always have him making the same move in the same position. It may be a perfect system—but a man doesn't play any game that way, damn it. He makes mistakes, he changes strategy. Even in a game this simple there'll be room for that. Most of all, a man *learns* a game as he plays it. He gets better as he goes along. That's what'll give Newton away, and that's what our bandit wants. It's probably heard about *aiyans*. Now as soon as it can be sure it's facing a dumb animal over there, and not a man or computer. . . ."

After a little while the Second Officer said: "I'm getting signals of their moves. They've begun play. Maybe we should've rigged up a board so we could follow along with the game."

"We better just be ready to go at it when the time comes." The Commander looked hopelessly at his salvo button, and then at the clock that showed two hours must pass before Gizmo could reasonably be hoped for.

Soon the Second Officer said: "That seems to be the end of the first game; Del lost it, if I'm reading their scoreboard signal right." He paused. "Sir, here's that signal we picked up the last time it turned the mind beam on. Del must be starting to get it again."

There was nothing for the Commander to say. The two men waited silently for the enemy's attack, hoping only that they could damage it in the seconds before it would overwhelm them and kill them.

"He's playing the second game," said the Second Officer, puzzled. "And I just heard him say 'Let's get on with it.' "

"His voice could be recorded. He must have made some plan of play for Newton to follow; but it won't fool the berserker for long. It can't."

Time crept unmeasurably past them.

The Second said: "He's lost the first four games. But he's *not* making the same moves every time. I wish we'd made a board. . . ."

"Shut up about the board! We'd be watching it instead of the panel. Now stay alert, Mister."

After what seemed a long time, the Second said: "Well, I'll be!"

"What?"

"Our side got a draw in that game."

"Then the beam can't be on him. Are you sure. . . ."

"It is! Look, here, the same indication we got last time. It's been on him the better part of an hour now, and getting stronger."

The Commander stared in disbelief; but he knew and trusted his Second's ability. And the panel indications were convincing. He said: "Then someone—or something—with no functioning mind is learning how to play a game, over there. Ha, ha," he added, as if trying to remember how to laugh.

The berserker won another game. Another draw. Another win for the enemy. Then three drawn games in a row.

Once the Second Officer heard Del's voice ask coolly: "Do you want to give up now?" On the next move he lost another game. But the following game ended in another draw. Del was plainly taking more time than his opponent to move, but not enough to make the enemy impatient.

"It's trying different modulations of the mind beam," said the Second. "And it's got the power turned way up."

"Yeah," said the Commander. Several times he had almost tried to radio Del, to say something that might keep the man's spirits up—and also to relieve his own feverish inactivity, and to try to find out what could possibly be going on. But he could not take the chance. Any interference might upset the miracle.

He could not believe the inexplicable success could last, even when the checker match turned gradually into an endless succession of drawn games between two perfect players. Hours ago the Commander had said good-bye to life and hope, and he still waited for the fatal moment.

And he waited.

"—not perish from the earth!" said Del Murray, and Newton's eager hands flew to loose his right arm from its shackle.

A game, unfinished on the little board before him, had been abandoned seconds earlier. The mind beam had been turned off at the same time, when Gizmo had burst into normal space right in position and only five minutes late; and the berserker had been forced to turn all its energies to meet the immediate all-out attack of Gizmo and Foxglove.

Del saw his computers, recovering from the effect of the beam, lock his aiming screen onto the berserker's scarred and bulging midsection, as he shot his right arm forward, scattering pieces from the game board.

"Checkmate!" he roared out hoarsely, and brought his fist down on the big red button.

"I'm glad it didn't want to play chess," Del said later, talking to the Commander in Foxglove's cabin. "I could never have rigged that up."

The ports were cleared now, and the men could look out at the cloud of expanding gas, still faintly luminous, that had been a berserker; metal fire-purged of the legacy of ancient evil.

But the Commander was watching Del. "You got Newt to play by following diagrams, I see that. But how could he *learn* the game?"

Del grinned. "He couldn't, but his toys could. Now wait before you slug me." He called the *aiyan* to him and took a small box from the animal's hand. The box rattled faintly as he held it up. On the cover was pasted a diagram of one possible position in the simplified checker game, with a different-colored arrow indicating each possible move of Del's pieces.

"It took a couple of hundred of these boxes," said Del. "This one was in the group that Newt examined for the fourth move. When he found a box with a diagram matching the position on the board, he picked the box up, pulled out one of these beads from inside, without looking—that was the hardest part to teach him in a hurry, by the way," said Del, demonstrating. "Ah, this one's blue. That means, make the move indicated on the cover by a blue arrow. Now the orange arrow leads to a poor position, see?" Del shook all the beads out of the box into his hand. "No orange beads left; there were six of each color when we started. But every time Newton drew a bead, he had orders to leave it out of the box until the game was over. Then, if the scoreboard indicated a loss for our side, he went back and threw away all the beads he had used. All the bad moves were gradually eliminated. In a few hours, Newt and his boxes learned to play the game perfectly.''

''Well,'' said the Commander. He thought for a moment, then reached down to scratch Newton behind the ears. ''I never would have come up with that idea.''

''I should have thought of it sooner. The basic idea's a couple of centuries old. And computers are supposed to be my business.''

''This could be a big thing,'' said the Commander. ''I mean your basic idea might be useful to any task force that has to face a berserker's mind beam.''

''Yeah.'' Del grew reflective. ''Also. . . .''

''What?''

''I was thinking of a guy I met once. Named Blankenship. I wonder if I *could* rig something up. . . .''

YES, I, THIRD HISTORIAN, have touched living minds, Earth minds, so deadly cool that for a while they could see war as a game. The first decades of the berserker war they were forced to see as a game being lost for life.

Nearly all the terrors of the slaughters in your past were present in this vaster war, all magnified in time and space. It was even less a game than any war has ever been.

As the grim length of the berserker war dragged on, even Earthmen discovered in it certain horrors that they had never known before.

Behold. . . .

GOODLIFE

"IT'S ONLY A MACHINE, Hemphill," said the dying man in a small voice.

Hemphill, drifting weightless in near-darkness, heard him with only faint contempt and pity. Let the wretch go out timidly, forgiving the universe everything, if he found the going-out easier that way!

Hemphill kept on staring out through the port, at the dark crenelated shape that blotted out so many of the stars.

There was probably just this one compartment of the passenger ship left livable, with three people in it, and the air whining out in steady leaks that would soon exhaust the emergency tanks. The ship was a wreck, torn and beaten, yet Hemphill's view of the enemy was steady. It must be a force of the enemy's that kept the wreck from spinning.

Now the young woman, another passenger, came drifting across the compartment to touch Hemphill on the arm. He thought her name was Maria something.

"Listen," she began. "Do you think we might—"

In her voice there was no despair, but the tone of planning; and so Hemphill had begun to listen to her. But she was interrupted.

The very walls of the cabin reverberated, driven like speaker diaphragms through the power of the enemy force field that still gripped the butchered hull. The quavering voice of the berserker machine came in:

"You who can still hear me, live on. I plan to spare you. I am sending a boat to save you from death."

Hemphill was sick with frustrated rage. He had never heard a berserker's voice in reality before, but still it was familiar as an old nightmare. He could feel the woman's hand pull away from his arm, and then he saw that in his rage he had raised both his hands to be claws, then fists that almost smashed themselves against the port. The damned thing wanted to take him inside it! Of all people in space it wanted to make him prisoner!

A plan rose instantly in his mind and flowed smoothly into action; he spun away from the port. There were warheads, for small defensive missiles, here in this compartment. He remembered seeing them.

The other surviving man, a ship's officer, dying slowly, bleeding through his uniform tatters, saw what Hemphill was doing in the wreckage, and drifted in front of him interferingly.

"You can't do that . . . you'll only destroy the boat it sends . . . if it lets you do that much . . . there may be other people . . . still alive here . . ."

The man's face had been upside-down before

Hemphill as the two of them drifted. As their movement let them see each other in normal position, the wounded man stopped talking, gave up and rotated himself away, drifting inertly as if already dead.

Hemphill could not hope to manage a whole warhead, but he could extract the chemical-explosive detonator, of a size to carry under one arm. All passengers had put on emergency spacesuits when the unequal battle had begun; now he found himself an extra air tank and some officer's laser pistol, which he stuck in a loop of his suit's belt.

The girl approached him again. He watched her warily.

"Do it," she said with quiet conviction, while the three of them spun slowly in the near-darkness, and the air leaks whined. "Do it. The loss of a boat will weaken it, a little, for the next fight. And we here have no chance anyway."

"Yes." He nodded approvingly. This girl understood what was important: to hurt a berserker, to smash, burn, destroy, to kill it finally. Nothing else mattered very much.

He pointed to the wounded mate, and whispered: "Don't let him give me away."

She nodded silently. It might hear them talking. If it could speak through these walls, it might be listening.

"A boat's coming," said the wounded man, in a calm and distant voice.

"Goodlife!" called the machine-voice, cracking between syllables as always.

"Here!" He woke up with a start, and got quickly to his feet. He had been dozing almost under the dripping end of a drinking-water pipe.

"Goodlife!" There were no speakers or scanners in

this little compartment; the call came from some distance away.

"Here!" He ran toward the call, his feet shuffling and thumping on metal. He had dozed off, being tired. Even though the battle had been a little one, there had been extra tasks for him, servicing and directing the commensal machines that roamed the endless ducts and corridors repairing damage. It was small help he could give, he knew.

Now his head and neck bore sore spots from the helmet he had had to wear; and his body was chafed in places from the unaccustomed covering he had to put on it when a battle came. This time, happily, there had been no battle damage at all.

He came to the flat glass eye of a scanner, and shuffled to a stop, waiting.

"Goodlife, the perverted machine has been destroyed, and the few badlives left are helpless."

"Yes!" He jiggled his body up and down in happiness.

"I remind you, life is evil," said the voice of the machine.

"Life is evil, I am Goodlife!" he said quickly, ceasing his jiggling. He did not think punishment impended, but he wanted to be sure.

"Yes. Like your parents before you, you have been useful. Now I plan to bring other humans inside myself, to study them closely. Your next use will be with them, in my experiments. I remind you, they are badlife. We must be careful."

"Badlife." He knew they were creatures shaped like himself, existing in the world beyond the machine. They caused the shudders and shocks and damage that made up a battle. "Badlife—here." It was a chilling thought. He raised his own hands and looked at them, then turned his attention up and down the passage in which he stood, trying to visualize the badlife become real before him.

"Go now to the medical room," said the machine. "You must be immunized against disease before you approach the badlife."

Hemphill made his way from one ruined compartment to another, until he found a gash in the outer hull that was plugged nearly shut. While he wrenched at the obstructing material he heard the clanging arrival of the berserker's boat, come for prisoners. He pulled harder, the obstruction gave way, and he was blown out into space.

Around the wreck were hundreds of pieces of flotsam, held near by tenuous magnetism or perhaps by the berserker's force fields. Hemphill found that his suit worked well enough. With its tiny jet he moved around the shattered hull of the passenger ship to where the berserker's boat had come to rest.

The dark blot of the berserker machine came into view against the starfield of deep space, battlemented like a fortified city of old, and larger than any such city had ever been. He could see that the berserker's boat had somehow found the right compartment and clamped itself to the wrecked hull. It would be gathering in Maria and the wounded man. Fingers on the plunger that would set off his bomb, Hemphill drifted closer.

On the brink of death, it annoyed him that he would never know with certainty that the boat was destroyed. And it was such a trifling blow to strike, such a small revenge.

Still drifting closer, holding the plunger ready, he

saw the puff of decompressed air moisture as the boat disconnected itself from the hull. The invisible force fields of the berserker surged, tugging at the boat, at Hemphill, at bits of wreckage within yards of the boat.

He managed to clamp himself to the boat before it was pulled away from him. He thought he had an hour's air in his suit tank, more than he would need.

As the berserker pulled him toward itself, Hemphill's mind hung over the brink of death, Hemphill's fingers gripped the plunger of his bomb. In his mind, his night-colored enemy was death. The black, scarred surface of it hurtled closer in the unreal starlight, becoming a planet toward which the boat fell.

Hemphill still clung to the boat when it was pulled into an opening that could have accommodated many ships. The size and power of the berserker were all around him, enough to overwhelm hate and courage alike.

His little bomb was a pointless joke. When the boat touched at a dark internal dock, Hemphill leaped away from it and scrambled to find a hiding place.

As he cowered on a shadowed ledge of metal, his hand wanted to fire the bomb, simply to bring death and escape. He forced his hand to be still. He forced himself to watch while the two human prisoners were sucked from the boat through a pulsing transparent tube that passed out of sight through a bulkhead. Not knowing what he meant to accomplish, he pushed himself in the direction of the tube. He glided through the dark enormous cavern almost weightlessly; the berserker's mass was enough to give it a small natural gravity of its own.

Within ten minutes he came upon an unmistakable airlock. It seemed to have been cut with a surrounding section of hull from some Earth warship and set into the bulkhead.

Inside an airlock would be as good a place for a bomb as he was likely to find. He got the outer door open and went in, apparently without triggering any alarms. If he destroyed himself here, he would deprive the berserker of—what? Why should it need an airlock at all?

Not for prisoners, thought Hemphill, if it sucks them in through a tube. Hardly an entrance built for enemies. He tested the air in the lock, and opened his helmet. For air-breathing friends, the size of men? That was a contradiction. Everything that lived and breathed must be a berserker's enemy, except the unknown beings who had built it. Or so man had thought, until now.

The inner door of the lock opened at Hemphill's push, and artificial gravity came on. He walked through into a narrow and badly lighted passage, his fingers ready on the plunger of his bomb.

"Go in, Goodlife," said the machine. "Look closely at each of them."

Goodlife made an uncertain sound in his throat, like a servomotor starting and stopping. He was gripped by a feeling that resembled hunger or the fear of punishment—because he was going to see life-forms directly now, not as old images on a stage. Knowing the reason for the unpleasant feeling did not help. He stood hesitating outside the door of the room where the bad-life was being kept. He had put on his suit again, as the machine had ordered. The suit would protect him if the badlife tried to damage him.

"Go in," the machine repeated.

"Maybe I'd better not," Goodlife said in misery, remembering to speak loudly and clearly. Punishment was always less likely when he did.

"Punish, punish," said the voice of the machine.

When it said the word twice, punishment was very near. As if already feeling in his bones the wrenching pain-that-left-no-damage, he opened the door quickly and stepped in.

He lay on the floor, bloody and damaged, in strange ragged suiting. And at the same time he was still in the doorway. His own shape was on the floor, the same human form he knew, but now seen entirely from outside. More than an image, far more, it was himself now bilocated. There, here, himself, not-himself—

Goodlife fell back against the door. He raised his arm and tried to bite it, forgetting his suit. He pounded his suited arms violently together, until there was bruised pain enough to nail him to himself where he stood.

Slowly, the terror subsided. Gradually his intellect could explain it and master it. This is me, here, here in the doorway. That, *there*, on the floor—that is another life. Another body, corroded like me with vitality. Only far worse than I. That one on the floor is badlife.

Maria Juarez had prayed continuously for a long time, her eyes closed. Cold impersonal grippers had moved her this way and that. Her weight had come back, and there was air to breathe when her helmet and her suit had been carefully removed. She opened her eyes and struggled when the grippers began to remove her inner coverall; she saw that she was in a low-ceilinged room, surrounded by man-sized machines of various shapes. When she struggled they gave up undressing her, chained her to the wall by one ankle, and glided away. The dying mate had been dropped at the other end of the room, as if not worth the trouble of further handling.

The man with the cold dead eyes, Hemphill, had tried to make a bomb, and failed. Now there would probably be no quick end to life—

When she heard the door open she opened her eyes again, to watch without comprehension, while the bearded young man in the ancient spacesuit went through senseless contortions in the doorway, and finally came forward to stand staring down at the dying man on the floor. The visitor's fingers moved with speed and precision when he raised his hands to the fasteners of his helmet; but the helmet's removal revealed ragged hair and beard framing a slack idiot's face.

He set the helmet down, then scratched and rubbed his shaggy head, never taking his eyes from the man on the floor. He had not yet looked once at Maria, and she could look nowhere but at him. She had never seen a face so blank on a living person. This was what happened to a berserker's prisoner!

And yet—and yet. Maria had seen brainwashed men before, ex-criminals on her own planet. She felt this man was something more—or something less.

The bearded man knelt beside the mate, with an air of hesitation, and reached out to touch him. The dying man stirred feebly, and looked up without comprehension. The floor under him was wet with blood.

The stranger took the mate's limp arm and bent it back and forth, as if interested in the articulation of the human elbow. The mate groaned, and struggled feebly. The stranger suddenly shot out his metal-gauntleted hands and seized the dying man by the throat.

Maria could not move, or turn her eyes away, though the whole room seemed to spin slowly, then faster and faster, around the focus of those armored hands.

The bearded man released his grip and stood erect, still watching the body at his feet.

"Turned off," he said distinctly.

Perhaps she moved. For whatever reason, the bearded man raised his sleepwalker's face to look at her. He did not meet her eyes, or avoid them. His eye movements were quick and alert, but the muscles of his face just hung there under the skin. He came toward her.

Why, he's young, she thought, hardly more than a boy. She backed against the wall and waited, standing. Women on her planet were not brought up to faint. Somehow, the closer he came, the less she feared him. But if he had smiled once, she would have screamed, on and on.

He stood before her, and reached out one hand to touch her face, her hair, her body. She stood still; she felt no lust in him, no meanness and no kindness. It was as if he radiated an emptiness.

"Not images," said the young man as if to himself. Then another word, sounding like: "Badlife."

Almost Maria dared to speak to him. The strangled man lay on the deck a few yards away.

The young man turned and shuffled deliberately away from her. She had never seen anyone who walked just like him. He picked up his helmet and went out the door without looking back.

A pipe streamed water into one corner of her little

space, where it gurgled away through a hole in the floor. The gravity seemed to be set at about Earth level. Maria sat leaning against the wall, praying and listening to her heart pound. It almost stopped when the door opened again, very slightly at first, then enough for a large cake of pink and green stuff that seemed to be food. The machine walked around the dead man on its way out.

She had eaten a little of the cake when the door opened again, very slightly at first, then enough for a man to step quickly in. It was Hemphill, the cold-eyed one from the ship, leaning a bit to one side as if dragged down by the weight of the little bomb he carried under his arm. After a quick look around he shut the door behind him and crossed the room to her, hardly glancing down as he stepped over the body of the mate.

"How many of them are there?" Hemphill whispered, bending over her. She had remained seated on the floor, too surprised to move or speak.

"Who?" she finally managed.

He jerked his head toward the door impatiently. "Them. The ones who live here inside *it*, and serve it. I saw one of them coming out of this room, when I was out in the passage. It's fixed up a lot of living space for them."

"I've only seen one man."

His eyes glinted at that. He showed Maria how the bomb could be made to explode, and gave it to her to hold, while he began to burn through her chain with his laser pistol. They exchanged information on what had happened. She did not think she would ever be able to set off the bomb and kill herself, but she did not tell that to Hemphill.

Just as they stepped out of the prison room, Hemphill

had a bad moment when three machines rolled toward them from around a corner. But the things ignored the two frozen humans and rolled silently past them, going on out of sight.

He turned to Maria with an exultant whisper: "The damned thing is three-quarters blind, here inside its own skin!"

She only waited, watching him with frightened eyes.

With the beginning of hope, a vague plan was forming in his mind. He led her along the passage, saying: "Now we'll see about that man. Or men." Was it too good to be true, that there was only one of them?

The corridors were badly lit, and full of uneven jogs and steps. Carelessly built concessions to life, he thought. He moved in the direction he had seen the man take.

After a few minutes of cautious advance, Hemphill heard the shuffling footsteps of one person ahead, coming nearer. He handed the bomb to Maria again, and pressed her behind him. They waited in a dark niche.

The footsteps approached with careless speed, a vague shadow bobbing ahead of them. The shaggy head swung so abruptly into view that Hemphill's metal-fisted swing was almost too late. The blow only grazed the back of the skull; the man yelped and staggered off balance and fell down. He was wearing an old-model spacesuit, with no helmet.

Hemphill crouched over him, shoving the laser pistol almost into his face. "Make a sound and I'll kill you. Where are the others?"

The face looking up at Hemphill was stunned—worse than stunned. It seemed more dead than alive, though the eyes moved alertly enough from Hemphill to Maria and back, disregarding the gun.

"He's the same one," Maria whispered.

"Where are your friends?" Hemphill demanded.

The man felt the back of his head, where he had been hit. "Damage," he said tonelessly, as if to himself. Then he reached up for the pistol, so calmly and steadily that he was nearly able to touch it.

Hemphill jumped back a step, and barely kept himself from firing. "Sit down or I'll kill you! Now tell me who you are, and how many others are here."

The man sat there calmly, with his putty face showing nothing. He said: "Your speech is steady in tone from word to word, not like that of the machine. You hold a killing tool there. Give it to me and I will destroy you and—that one."

It seemed this man was only a brainwashed ruin, instead of an unspeakable traitor. Now what use could be made of him? Hemphill moved back another step, slowly lowering the pistol.

Maria spoke to their prisoner. "Where are you from? What planet?"

A blank stare.

"Your home," she persisted. "Where were you born?"

"From the birth tank." Sometimes the tones of the man's voice shifted like the berserker's, as if he was a fearful comedian mocking it.

Hemphill gave an unstable laugh. "From a birth tank, of course. What else? Now for the last time, where are the others?"

"I do not understand."

Hemphill sighed. "All right. Where's this birth tank?" He had to start with something.

The place looked like the storeroom of a biology lab,

badly lighted, piled and crowded with equipment, laced with pipes and conduits. Probably no living technician had ever worked here.

"You were *born* here?" Hemphill demanded.

"Yes."

"He's crazy."

"No. Wait." Maria's voice sank to an even lower whisper, as if she was frightened anew. She took the hand of the slack-faced man. He bent his head to stare at their touching hands.

"Do you have a name?" she asked, as if speaking to a lost child.

"I am Goodlife."

"I think it's hopeless," put in Hemphill.

The girl ignored him. "Goodlife? My name is Maria. And this is Hemphill."

No reaction.

"Who were your parents? Father? Mother?"

"They were goodlife too. They helped the machine. There was a battle, and badlife killed them. But they had given cells of their bodies to the machine, and from those cells it made me. Now I am the only goodlife."

"Great God," whispered Hemphill.

Silent, awed attention seemed to move Goodlife when threats and pleas had not. His face twisted in awkward grimaces; he turned to stare into a corner. Then, for almost the first time, he volunteered a communication: "I know they were like you. A man and a woman."

Hemphill wanted to sweep every cubic foot of the miles of mechanism with his hatred; he looked around at every side and angle of the room.

"The damned things," he said, his voice cracking

like the berserker's. "What they've done to me. To you. To everyone."

Plans seemed to come to him when the strain of hating was greatest. He moved quickly to put a hand on Goodlife's shoulder. "Listen to me. Do you know what a radioactive isotope is?"

"Yes."

"There will be a place, somewhere, where the—the machine decided what it will do next—what strategy to follow. A place holding a block of some isotope with a long half-life. Probably near the center of the machine. Do you know of such a place?"

"Yes, I know where the strategic housing is."

"Strategic housing." Hope mounted to a strong new level. "Is there a way for us to reach it?"

"You are badlife!" He knocked Hemphill's hand away, awkwardly. "You want to damage the machine, and you have damaged me. You are to be destroyed."

Maria took over, trying to soothe. "Goodlife—we are not bad, this man and I. Those who built this machine are the badlife. Someone built it, you know, some living people built it, long ago. They were the real badlife."

"Badlife." He might be agreeing with Maria, or accusing her.

"Don't you want to live, Goodlife? Hemphill and I want to live. We want to help you, because you're alive, like us. Won't you help us now?"

Goodlife was silent for a few moments, contemplating a bulkhead. Then he turned back to face them and said: "All life thinks it is, but it is not. There are only particles, energy and space, and the laws of the machines."

Maria kept at him. "Goodlife, listen to me. A wise man once said: 'I think, therefore I am.' "

"A wise man?" he questioned, in his cracking voice. Then he sat down on the deck, hugging his knees and rocking back and forth. He might be thinking.

Drawing Maria aside, Hemphill said: "You know, we have a faint hope now. There's plenty of air in here, there's water and food. There are warships following this thing, there must be. If we can find a way to disable it, we can wait and maybe be picked up in a month or two. Or less."

She watched him silently for a moment. "Hemphill—what have these machines done to you?"

"My wife—my children." He thought his voice sounded almost indifferent. "They were on Pascalo, three years ago; there was nothing left. This machine, or one like it."

She took his hand, as she had taken Goodlife's. They both looked down at the joined fingers, then raised their eyes, smiling briefly together at the similarity of action.

"Where's the bomb?" Hemphill thought aloud suddenly, spinning around.

It lay in a dim corner. He grabbed it up again, and strode over to where Goodlife sat rocking back and forth.

"Well, are you with us? Us, or the ones who built the machine?"

Goodlife stood up, and looked closely at Hemphill. "They were inspired by the laws of physics, which controlled their brains, to build the machine. Now the machine has preserved them as images. It has preserved my father and mother, and it will preserve me."

"What images do you mean? Where are they?"

32

"The images in the theater."

It seemed best to accustom this creature to cooperation, to win his confidence and at the same time learn
about him and the machine. Then, on to the strategic
housing. Hemphill made his voice friendly: "Will you
guide us to the theater, Goodlife?"

It was by far the largest air-filled room they had yet
found, and held a hundred seats of a shape usable by
Earth-descended men, though Hemphill knew it had
been built for someone else. The theater was elabo-
rately furnished and well-lighted. When the door
closed behind them, the ranked images of intelligent
creatures brightened into life upon the stage.

The stage became a window into a vast hall. One
person stood forward at an imaged lectern; he was a
slender, fine-boned being, topologically like a man
except for the single eye that stretched across his face,
with a bright bulging pupil that slid to and fro like
mercury.

The speaker's voice was a high-pitched torrent of
clicks and whines. Most of those in the ranks behind
him wore a kind of uniform. When he paused, they
whined in unison.

"What does he say?" Maria whispered.

Goodlife looked at her. "The machine has told me
that it has lost the meaning of the sounds."

"Then may we see the images of your parents,
Goodlife?"

Hemphill, watching the stage, started to object; but
the girl was right. The sight of this fellow's parents
might be more immediately helpful.

Goodlife found a control somewhere.

Hemphill was surprised momentarily that the parents

appeared only in flat projected pictures. First the man was there, against a plain background, blue eyes and neat short beard, nodding his head with a pleasant expression on his face. He wore the lining coverall of a spacesuit.

Then the woman, holding some kind of cloth before her for covering, and looking straight into the camera. She had a broad face and red braided hair. There was hardly time to see anything more before the alien orator was back, whining faster than ever.

Hemphill turned to ask: "Is that all? All you know of your parents?"

"Yes. The badlife killed them. Now they are images, they no longer think they exist."

Maria thought the creature in the projection was assuming a more didactic tone. Three-dimensional charts of stars and planets appeared near him, one after another, and he gestured at them as he spoke. He had vast numbers of stars and planets on his charts to boast about; she could tell somehow that he was boasting.

Hemphill was moving toward the stage a step at a time, more and more absorbed. Maria did not like the way the light of the images reflected on his face.

Goodlife, too, watched the stage pageant which perhaps he had seen a thousand times before. Maria could not tell what thoughts might be passing behind his meaningless face which had never had another human face to imitate. On impulse she took his arm again.

"Goodlife, Hemphill and I are alive, like you. Will you help us now, to stay alive? Then in the future we will always help you." She had a sudden mental picture of Goodlife rescued, taken to a planet, cowering among the staring badlife.

"Good. Bad." His hand reached to take hold of hers; he had removed his suit gauntlets. He swayed back and forth as if she attracted and repelled him at the same time. She wanted to scream and wail for him, to tear apart with her fingers the mindlessly proceeding metal that had made him what he was.

"We've got them!" It was Hemphill, coming back from the stage, where the recorded tirade went on unrelentingly. He was exultant. "Don't you see? He's showing what must be a complete catalogue, of every star and rock they own. It's a victory speech. But when we study those charts we can find them, we can track them down and *reach* them!"

"Hemphill." She wanted to calm him back to concentration on immediate problems. "How old are those images up there? What part of the galaxy were they made in? Or do they even come from some other galaxy? Will we ever be able to tell?"

Hemphill lost some of his enthusiasm. "Anyway, it's a chance to track them down; it's information we've got to save." He pointed at Goodlife. "He's got to take me to what he calls the strategic housing; then we can sit and wait for the warships, or maybe get off this damned thing in a boat."

She stroked Goodlife's hand, soothing a baby. "Yes, but he's confused. How could he be anything else?"

"Of course." Hemphill paused to consider. "You can handle him much better than I."

She didn't answer.

Hemphill went on: "Now you're a woman, and he

appears to be a physically healthy young male. Calm him down if you like, but somehow you've *got* to persuade him to help me. Everything depends on it." He had turned toward the stage again, unable to take more than half his mind from the star charts. "Go for a little walk and talk with him; don't get far away."

And what else was there to do? She led Goodlife from the theater while the dead man on the stage clicked and shouted, cataloguing his thousand suns.

Too much had happened, was still happening, and all at once he could no longer stand to be near the badlife. Goodlife found himself pulling away from the female, running, flying down the passages, toward the place where he had fled when he was small and strange fears had come from nowhere. It was the room where the machine always saw and heard him, and was ready to talk to him.

He stood before the attention of the machine, in the chamber-that-has-shrunk. He thought of the place so, because he could remember it clearly as a larger room, where the scanners and speakers of the machine towered above his head. He knew the real change had been his own physical growth; still, this compartment was set apart in a special association with food and sleep and protective warmth.

"I have listened to the badlife, and shown them things," he confessed, fearing punishment.

"I know that, Goodlife, for I have watched. These things have become a part of my experiment."

What joyous relief! The machine said nothing of punishment, though it must know that the words and actions of the badlife had shaken and confused his own ideas. He had even imagined himself showing the man Hemphill the strategic housing, and so putting an end to all punishment, for always.

"They wanted me—they wanted me to—"

"I have watched. I have listened. The man is tough and evil, powerfully motivated to fight against me. I must understand his kind, for they cause much damage. He must be tested to his limits, to destruction. He believes himself free inside me, and so he will not think as a prisoner. This is important."

Goodlife pulled off his irritating suit; the machine would not let the badlife in here. He sank down to the floor and wrapped his arms around the base of the scanner-speaker console. Once long ago the machine had given him a thing that was soft and warm when he held it . . . he closed his eyes.

"What are my orders?" he asked sleepily. Here in this chamber all was steady and comforting, as always.

"First, do not tell the badlife of these orders. Then, do what the man Hemphill tells you to do. No harm will come to me."

"He has a bomb."

"I watched his approach, and I disabled his bomb, even before he entered to attack me. His pistol can do me no serious harm. Do you think one badlife can conquer me?"

"No." Smiling, reassured, he curled into a more comfortable position. "Tell me about my parents." He had heard the story a thousand times, but it was always good.

"Your parents were good, they gave themselves to me. Then, during a great battle, the badlife killed them. The badlife hated them, as they hate you. When they say they like you, they lie, with the evil untruth of all badlife.

"But your parents were good, and each gave me a part of their bodies, and from the parts I made you. Your parents were destroyed completely by the badlife, or I would have saved even their non-functioning bodies for you to see. That would have been good."

"Yes."

"The two badlife have searched for you. Now they are resting. Sleep, Goodlife."

He slept.

Awakening, he remembered a dream in which two people had beckoned him to join them on the stage of the theater. He knew they were his mother and father, though they looked like the two badlife. The dream faded before his waking mind could grasp it firmly.

He ate and drank, while the machine talked to him.

"If the man Hemphill wants to be guided to the strategic housing, take him there. I will capture him there, and let him escape later to try again. When finally he can be provoked to fight no more, I will destroy him. But I mean to preserve the life of the female. You and she will produce more goodlife for me."

"Yes!" It was immediately clear what a good thing that would be. They would give parts of their bodies to the machine, so new goodlife bodies could be built, cell by cell. And the man Hemphill, who punished and damaged with his fast-swinging arm, would be utterly destroyed.

When he rejoined the badlife, the man Hemphill barked questions and threatened punishment until Goodlife was confused and a little frightened. But

Goodlife agreed to help, and was careful to reveal nothing of what the machine planned. Maria was more pleasant than ever. He touched her whenever he could.

Hemphill demanded to be taken to the strategic housing. Goodlife agreed at once; he had been there many times. There was a high-speed elevator that made the fifty mile journey easy.

Hemphill paused, before saying: "You're too damn willing, all of a sudden." Turning his face to Maria. "I don't trust him."

This badlife thought he was being false! Goodlife was angered; the machine never lied, and no properly obedient goodlife could lie.

Hemphill paced around, and finally demanded: "Is there any route that approaches this strategic housing in such a way that the machine cannot possibly watch us?"

Goodlife thought. "I believe there is one such way. We will have to carry extra tanks of air, and travel many miles through vacuum." The machine had said to help Hemphill, and help he would. He hoped he could watch when the male badlife was finally destroyed.

There had been a battle, perhaps fought while men on Earth were hunting the mammoth with spears. The berserker had met some terrible opponent, and had taken a terrible lance-thrust of a wound. A cavity two miles wide at the widest, and fifty miles deep, had been driven in by a sequence of shaped atomic charges, through level after level of machinery, deck after deck of armor, and had been stopped only by the last inner defenses of the buried unliving heart. The berserker had survived, and crushed its enemy, and soon afterward its repair machines had sealed over the outer opening of the wound, using extra thicknesses of armor. It had meant to gradually rebuild the whole destruction; but there was so much life in the galaxy, and so much of it was stubborn and clever. Somehow battle damage accumulated faster than it could be repaired. The huge hole was used as a conveyor path, and never much worked on.

When Hemphill saw the blasted cavity—what little of it his tiny suit lamp could show—he felt a shrinking fear that was greater than any in his memory. He stopped on the edge of the void, drifting there with his arm instinctively around Maria. She had put on a suit and accompanied him, without being asked, without protest or eagerness.

They had already come an hour's journey from the airlock, through weightless vacuum inside the great machine. Goodlife had led the way through section after section, with every show of cooperation. Hemphill had the pistol ready, and the bomb, and two hundred feet of cord tied around his left arm.

But when Hemphill recognized the once-molten edge of the berserker's great scar for what it was, his delicate new hope of survival left him. This, the damned thing had survived. This, perhaps, had hardly weakened it. Again, the bomb under his arm was only a pathetic toy.

Goodlife drifted up to them. Hemphill had already taught him to touch helmets for speech in vacuum.

"This great damage is the one path we can take to reach the strategic housing without passing scanners or service machines. I will teach you to ride the conveyor. It will carry us most of the way."

The conveyor was a thing of force fields and huge rushing containers, hundreds of yards out in the enormous wound and running lengthwise through it. When the conveyor's force fields caught the people up, their weightlessness felt more than ever like falling, with occasional vast shapes, corpuscles of the berserker's bloodstream, flickering past in the near-darkness to show their speed of movement.

Hemphill flew beside Maria, holding her hand. Her face was hard to see, inside her helmet.

This conveyor was yet another mad new world, a fairy tale of monsters and flying and falling. Hemphill fell past his fear into a new determination. I can do it, he thought. The thing is blind and helpless here. I will do it, and I will survive if I can.

Goodlife led them from the slowing conveyor, to drift into a chamber hollowed in the inner armor by the final explosion at the end of the ancient lance-thrust. The chamber was an empty sphere a hundred feet across, from which cracks radiated out into the solid armor. On the surface nearest the center of the berserker, one fissure was as wide as a door, where the last energy of the enemy's blow had driven ahead.

Goodlife touched helmets with Hemphill, and said: "I have seen the other end of this crack, from inside, at the strategic housing. It is only a few yards from here."

Hemphill hesitated for only a moment, wondering whether to send Goodlife through the twisting passage first. But if this was some incredibly complex trap, the trigger of it might be anywhere.

He touched his helmet to Maria's. "Stay behind him. Follow him through and keep an eye on him." Then Hemphill led the way.

The fissure narrowed as he followed it, but at its end it was still wide enough for him to force himself through.

He had reached another vast hollow sphere, the inner temple. In the center was a complexity the size of a small house, shock-mounted on a web of girders that ran from it in every direction. This could be nothing but the strategic housing. There was a glow from it like flickering moonlight; force field switches responding to the random atomic turmoil within, somehow choosing what human shipping lane or colony would be next attacked, and how.

Hemphill felt a pressure rising in his mind and soul, toward a climax of triumphal hate. He drifted forward, cradling his bomb tenderly, starting to unwind the cord wrapped around his arm. He tied the free end delicately to the plunger of the bomb, as he approached the central complex.

I mean to live, he thought, to watch the damned thing die. I will tape the bomb against the central block, that so-innocent looking slab in there, and I will brace myself around two hundred feet of these heavy metal corners, and pull the cord.

Goodlife stood braced in the perfect place from which to see the heart of the machine, watching the man Hemphill string his cord. Goodlife felt a certain satisfaction that his prediction had been right, that the strategic housing was approachable by this one narrow path of the great damage. They would not have to go back that way. When the badlife had been captured, all of them could ride up in the air-filled elevator Goodlife used when he came here for maintenance practice.

Hemphill had finished stringing his cord. Now he waved his arm at Goodlife and Maria, who clung to the same girder, watching. Now Hemphill pulled on the cord. Of course, nothing happened. The machine had said the bomb was disabled, and the machine would make very certain in such a matter.

Maria pushed away from beside Goodlife, and drifted in toward Hemphill.

Hemphill tugged again and again on his cord. Goodlife sighed impatiently, and moved. There was a great cold in the girders here; he could begin to feel it now through the fingers and toes of his suit.

At last, when Hemphill started back to see what was wrong with his device, the service machines came from where they had been hiding, to seize him. He tried to draw his pistol, but their grippers moved far too quickly.

It was hardly a struggle that Goodlife saw, but he watched with interest. Hemphill's figure had gone rigid in the suit, obviously straining every muscle to the limit. Why should the badlife try to struggle against steel and atomic power? The machines bore the man effortlessly away, toward the elevator shaft. Goodlife felt an uneasiness.

Maria was drifting, her face turned back toward Goodlife. He wanted to go to her and touch her again, but suddenly he was a little afraid, as before when he had run from her. One of the service machines came back from the elevator to grip her and carry her away. She kept her face turned toward Goodlife. He turned away from her, a feeling like punishment in the core of his being.

In the great cold silence, the flickering light from the

strategic housing bathed everything. In the center, a chaotic block of atoms. Elsewhere, engines, relays, sensing units. Where was it, really, the mighty machine that spoke to him? Everywhere, and nowhere. Would these new feelings, brought by the badlife, ever leave him? He tried to understand himself, and could not begin.

Light flickered on a round shape a few yards away among the girders, a shape that offended Goodlife's sense of the proper and necessary in machinery. Looking closer, he saw it was a space helmet.

The motionless figure was wedged only lightly in an angle between frigid metal beams, but there was no force in here to move it.

He could hear the suit creak, stiff with great cold, when he grabbed it and turned it. Unseeing blue eyes looked out at Goodlife through the faceplate. The man's face wore a neat short beard.

"Ahhh, yes," sighed Goodlife inside his own helmet. A thousand times he had seen the image of this face.

His father had been carrying something, heavy, strapped carefully to his ancient suit. His father had carried it this far, and here the old suit had wheezed and failed.

His father, too, had followed the logical narrow path of the great damage, to reach the strategic housing without being seen. His father had choked and died and frozen here, carrying toward the strategic housing what could only be a bomb.

Goodlife heard his own voice keening, without words, and he could not see plainly for the tears floating in his helmet. His fingers felt numbered with cold as he unstrapped the bomb and lifted it from his father. . . .

Hemphill was too exhausted to do more than gasp as the service machine carried him out of the elevator and along the air-filled corridor toward the prison room. When the machine went dead and dropped him, he had to lie still for long seconds before he could attack it again. It had hidden his pistol somewhere, so he began to beat on the robotlike thing with his armored fists, while it stood unresisting. Soon it toppled over. Hemphill sat on it and beat it some moer, cursing it with sobbing breaths.

It was nearly a minute later when the tremor of the explosion, racing from the compounded chaos of the berserker's torn-out heart, racing through metal beams and decks, reached the corridor, where it was far too faint for anyone to feel.

Maria, completely weary, sat where her metal captor had dropped her, watching Hemphill, loving him in a way, and pitying him.

He stopped his pointless pounding of the machine under him, and said hoarsely: "It's a trick, another damned trick."

The tremor had been too faint for anyone to feel, here, but Maria shook her head. "No, I don't think so." She saw that power still seemed to be on the elevator, and she watched the door of it.

Hemphill went away to search among the now-purposeless machines for weapons and food. He came back, raging again. What was probably an automatic destructor charge had wrecked the theater and the star-charts. They might as well see about getting away in the boat.

She ignored him, still watching an elevator door which never opened. Soon she began quietly to cry.

The terror of the berserkers spread ahead of them across the galaxy. Even on worlds not touched by the physical fighting, there were people who felt themselves breathing darkness, and sickened inwardly. Few men on any world chose to look for long out into the nighttime sky. Some men on each world found themselves newly obsessed by the shadows of death.

I touched a mind whose soul was dead. . . .

PATRON OF THE ARTS

AFTER SOME HOURS' work, Herron found himself hungry and willing to pause for food. Looking over what he had just done, he could easily imagine one of the sycophantic critics praising it: A huge canvas, of discordant and brutal line! Aflame with a sense of engulfing menace! And for once, Herron thought, the critic might be praising something good.

Turning away from his view of easel and blank bulkhead, Herron found that his captor had moved up silently to stand only an arm's length behind him, for all the world like some human kibitzer.

He had to chuckle. "I suppose you've some idiotic suggestion to make?"

The roughly man-shaped machine said nothing, though it had what might be a speaker mounted on what might be a face. Herron shrugged and walked around it, going forward in search of the galley. This ship had been only a few hours out from Earth on C-plus drive when the berserker machine had run it down and captured it; and Piers Herron, the only passenger, had not yet had time to learn his way around.

It was more than a galley, he saw when he reached it—it was meant to be a place where arty colonial ladies could sit and twitter over tea when they grew weary of staring at pictures. The *Frans Hals* had been built as a traveling museum; then the war of life against berserker machines had grown hot around Sol, and BuCulture had wrongly decided that Earth's art treasures would be safer if shipped away to Tau Epsilon. The *Frans* was ideally suited for such a mission, and for almost nothing else.

Looking further forward from the entrance to the galley, Herron could see that the door to the crew compartment had been battered down, but he did not go to look inside. Not that it would bother him to look, he told himself; he was as indifferent to horror as he was to almost all other human things. The *Frans'* crew of two were in there, or what was left of them after they had tried to fight off the berserker's boarding machines. Doubtless they had preferred death to capture.

Herron preferred nothing. Now he was probably the only living being—apart from a few bacteria—within half a light year; and he was pleased to discover that his situation did not terrify him; that his long-growing weariness of life was not just a pose to fool himself.

His metal captor followed him into the galley, watching while he set the kitchen devices to work.

"Still no suggestions?" Herron asked it. "Maybe you're smarter than I thought."

"I am what men call a berserker," the man-shaped thing squeaked at him suddenly, in an ineffectual-

48

sounding voice. "I have captured your ship, and I will talk with you through this small machine you see. Do you grasp my meaning?"

"I understand as well as I need to." Herron had not yet seen the berserker itself, but he knew it was probably drifting a few miles away, or a few hundred or a thousand miles, from the ship it had captured. Captain Hanus had tried desperately to escape it, diving the *Frans* into a cloud of dark nebula where no ship or machine could move faster than light, and where the advantage in speed lay with the smaller hull.

The chase had been at speeds up to a thousand miles a second. Forced to remain in normal space, the berserker could not steer its bulk among the meteoroids and gas-wisps as well as the *Frans's* radar-computer system could maneuver the fleeing ship. But the berserker had sent an armed launch of its own to take up the chase, and the weaponless *Frans* had had no chance.

Now, dishes of food, hot and cold, popped out on a galley table, and Herron bowed to the machine. "Will you join me?"

"I need no organic food."

Herron sat down with a sigh. "In the end," he told the machine, "you'll find that lack of humor is as pointless as laughter. Wait and see if I'm not right." He began to eat, and found himself not so hungry as he had thought. Evidently his body still feared death—this surprised him a little.

"Do you normally function in the operation of this ship?" the machine asked.

"No," he said, making himself chew and swallow. "I'm not much good at pushing buttons." A peculiar thing that had happened was nagging at Herron. When capture was only minutes away, Captain Hanus had come dashing aft from the control room, grabbing Herron and dragging him along in a tearing hurry, aft past all the stored art treasures.

"Herron, listen—if we don't make it, see here?" Tooling open a double hatch in the stern compartment, the captain had pointed into what looked like a short padded tunnel, the diameter of a large drainpipe. "The regular lifeboat won't get away, but this might."

"Are you waiting for the Second Officer, Captain, or leaving us now?"

"There's room for only one, you fool, and I'm not the one who's going."

"You mean to save me? Captain, I'm touched!" Herron laughed, easily and naturally. "But don't put yourself out."

"You idiot. Can I trust you?" Hanus lunged into the boat, his hands flying over its controls. Then he backed out, glaring like a madman. "Listen. Look here. This button is the activator; now I've set things up so the boat should come out in the main shipping lanes and start sending a distress signal. Chances are she'll be picked up safely then. Now the controls are set, only this activator button needs to be pushed down—"

The berserker's launch had attacked at that moment, with a roar like mountains falling on the hull of the ship. The lights and artificial gravity had failed and then come abruptly back. Piers Herron had been thrown on his side, his wind knocked out. He had watched while the captain, regaining his feet and moving like a man in a daze, had closed the hatch on the mysterious little boat again and staggered forward to his control room.

"Why are you here?" the machine asked Herron.

He dropped the forkful of food he had been staring at. He didn't have to hesitate before answering the question. "Do you know what BuCulture is? They're the fools in charge of art, on Earth. Some of them, like a lot of other fools, think I'm a great painter. They worship me. When I said I wanted to leave Earth on this ship, they made it possible.

"I wanted to leave because almost everything that is worthwhile in any true sense is being removed from Earth. A good part of it is on this ship. What's left behind on the planet is only a swarm of animals, breeding and dying, fighting—"

"Why did you not try to fight or hide when my machines boarded this ship?"

"Because it would have done no good."

When the berserker's prize crew had forced their way in through an airlock, Herron had been setting up his easel in what was to have been a small exhibition hall, and he had paused to watch the uninvited visitors file past. One of the man-shaped metal things, the one through which he was being questioned now, had stayed to stare at him through its lenses while the others had moved on forward to the crew compartment.

"Herron!" The intercom had shouted. "Try, Herron, please! You know what to do!" Clanging noises followed, and gunshots and curses.

What to do, Captain? Why, yes. The shock of events and the promise of imminent death had stirred up some kind of life in Piers Herron. He looked with interest at the alien shapes and lines of his inanimate captor, the inhuman cold of deep space frosting over its metal here in the warm cabin. Then he turned away from it and began to paint the berserker, trying to catch not the outward shape he had never seen, but what he felt of its inwardness. He felt the emotionless deadliness of its watching lenses, boring into his back. The sensation was faintly pleasurable, like cold spring sunshine.

"What is good?" the machine asked Herron, standing over him in the galley while he tried to eat.

He snorted. "You tell me."

It took him literally. "To serve the cause of what men call death is good. To destroy life is good."

Herron pushed his nearly full plate into a disposal slot and stood up. "You're almost right about life being worthless—but even if you were entirely right, why so enthusiastic? What is there praiseworthy about death?" Now his thoughts surprised him as his lack of appetite had.

"I am entirely right," said the machine.

For long seconds Herron stood still, as if thinking, though his mind was almost completely blank. "No," he said finally, and waited for a bolt to strike him.

"In what do you think I am wrong?" it asked.

"I'll show you." He led it out of the galley, his hands sweating and his mouth dry. Why wouldn't the damned thing kill him and have done?

The paintings were racked row on row and tier on tier; there was no room in the ship for more than a few to be displayed in a conventional way. Herron found the drawer he wanted and pulled it open so the portrait inside swung into full view, lights springing on around it to bring out the rich colors beneath the twentieth-century statglass coating.

"This is where you're wrong," Herron said.

The man-shaped thing's scanner studied the portrait

for perhaps fifteen seconds. "Explain what you are showing me," it said.

"I bow to you!" Herron did so. "You admit ignorance! You even ask an intelligible question, if one that is somewhat too broad. First, tell me what *you* see here."

"I see the image of a life-unit, its third spatial dimension of negligible size as compared to the other two. The image is sealed inside a protective jacket transparent to the wavelengths used by the human eye. The life-unit imaged is, or was, an adult male apparently in good functional condition, garmented in a manner I have not seen before. What I take to be one garment is held before him—"

"You see a man with a glove," Herron cut in, wearying of his bitter game. "That is the title, *Man with a Glove*. Now what do you say about it?"

There was a pause of twenty seconds. "Is it an attempt to praise life, to say that life is good?"

Looking now at Titian's thousand-year-old more-than-masterpiece, Herron hardly heard the machine's answer; he was thinking helplessly and hopelessly of his own most recent work.

"Now you will tell me what it means," said the machine without emphasis.

Herron walked away without answering, leaving the drawer open.

The berserker's mouthpiece walked at his side. "Tell me what it means or you will be punished."

"If you can pause to think, so can I." But Herron's stomach had knotted up at the threat of punishment, seeming to feel that pain mattered even more than death. Herron had great contempt for his stomach.

53

His feet took him back to his easel. Looking at the discordant and brutal line that a few minutes ago had pleased him, he now found it as disgusting as everything else he had tried to do in the past year.

The berserker asked: "What have you made here?"

Herron picked up a brush he had forgotten to clean, and wiped at it irritably. "It is my attempt to get at your essence, to capture you with paint and canvas as you have seen those humans captured." He waved at the storage racks. "My attempt has failed, as most do."

There was another pause, which Herron did not try to time.

"An attempt to praise me?"

Herron broke the spoiled brush and threw it down. "Call it what you like."

This time the pause was short, and at its end the machine did not speak, but turned away and walked in the direction of the airlock. Some of its fellows clanked past to join it. From the direction of the airlock there began to come sounds like those of heavy metal being worked and hammered. The interrogation seemed to be over for the time being.

Herron's thoughts wanted to be anywhere but on his work or on his fate, and they returned to what Hanus had shown him, or tried to show him. Not a regular lifeboat, but she might get away, the captain had said. All it needs now is to press the button.

Herron started walking, smiling faintly as he realized that if the berserker was as careless as it seemed, he might possibly escape it.

Escape to what? He couldn't paint any more, if he ever could. All that really mattered to him now was here, and on other ships leaving Earth.

Back at the storage rack, Herron swung the *Man with a Glove* out so its case came free from the rack and became a handy cart. He wheeled the portrait aft. There might be yet one worthwhile thing he could do with his life.

The picture was massive in its statglass shielding, but he thought he could fit it into the boat.

As an itch might nag a dying man, the question of what the captain had been intending with the boat nagged Herron. Hanus hadn't seemed worried about Herron's fate, but instead had spoken of trusting Herron. . . .

Nearing the stern, out of sight of the machines, Herron passed a strapped-down stack of crated statuary, and heard a noise, a rapid feeble pounding.

It took several minutes to find and open the proper case. When he lifted the lid with its padded lining, a girl wearing a coverall sat up, her hair all wild as if standing in terror.

"Are they gone?" She had bitten at her fingers and nails until they were bleeding. When he didn't answer at once, she repeated her question again and again, in a rising whine.

"The machines are still here," he said at last.

Literally shaking in her fear, she climbed out of the case. "Where's Gus? Have they taken him?"

"Gus?" But he thought he was beginning to understand.

"Gus Hanus, the captain. He and I are—he was trying to save me, to get me away from Earth."

"I'm quite sure he's dead," said Herron. "He fought the machines."

Her bleeding fingers clutched at her lower face.

"They'll kill us, too! Or worse! What can we do?"

"Don't mourn your lover so deeply," he said. But the girl seemed not to hear him; her wild eyes looked this way and that, expecting the machines. "Help me with this picture," he told her calmly. "Hold the door there for me."

She obeyed as if half-hypnotized, not questioning what he was doing.

"Gus said there'd be a boat," she muttered to herself. "If he had to smuggle me down to Tau Epsilon he was going to use a special little boat—" She broke off, staring at Herron, afraid that he had heard her and was going to steal her boat. As indeed he was.

When he had the painting in the stern compartment, he stopped. He looked long at the *Man with a Glove*, but in the end all he could seem to see was that the fingertips of the ungloved hand were not bitten bloody.

Herron took the shivering girl by the arm and pushed her into the tiny boat. She huddled there in dazed terror; she was not good-looking. He wondered what Hanus had seen in her.

"There's room for only one," he said, and she shrank and bared her teeth as if afraid he meant to drag her out again. "After I close the hatch, push that button there, the activator. Understand?

That she understood at once. He dogged the double hatch shut and waited. Only about three seconds passed before there came a scraping sound that he supposed meant the boat had gone.

Nearby was a tiny observation blister, and Herron put his head into it and watched the stars turn beyond the dark blizzard of the nebula. After a while he saw the berserker through the blizzard, turning with the stars, black and rounded and bigger than any mountain. It gave no sign that it had detected the tiny boat slipping away. Its launch was very near the *Frans* but none of its commensal machines were in sight.

Looking the *Man with a Glove* in the eye, Herron pushed him forward again, to a spot near his easel. The discordant lines of Herron's own work were now worse than disgusting, but Herron made himself work on them.

He hadn't time to do much before the man-shaped machine came walking back to him; the uproar of metalworking had ceased. Wiping his brush carefully, Herron put it down, and nodded at his berserker portrait. "When you destroy all the rest, save this painting. Carry it back to those who built you, they deserve it."

The machine-voice squeaked back at him: "Why do you think I will destroy paintings? Even if they are attempts to praise life, they are dead things in themselves, and so in themselves they are good."

Herron was suddenly too frightened and weary to speak. Looking dully into the machine's lenses he saw there tiny flickerings, keeping time with his own pulse and breathing, like the indications of a lie detector.

"Your mind is divided," said the machine. "But with its much greater part you have praised me. I have repaired your ship, and set its course. I now release you, so other life-units can learn from you to praise what is good."

Herron could only stand there staring straight ahead of him, while a trampling of metal feet went past, and there was a final scraping on the hull.

After some time he realized he was alive and free.

At first he shrank from the dead men, but after once touching them he soon got them into a freezer. He had no particular reason to think either of them Believers, but he found a book and read Islamic, Ethical, Christian and Jewish burial services.

Then he found an undamaged handgun on the deck, and went prowling the ship, taken suddenly with the wild notion that a machine might have stayed behind. Pausing only to tear down the abomination from his easel, he went on to the very stern. There he had to stop, facing the direction in which he supposed the berserker now was.

"Damn you, I can change!" he shouted at the stern bulkhead. His voice broke. "I can paint again. I'll show you . . . I can change. I am alive."

Different men will find different ways of praising life, of calling it good.

Even I, who by my nature cannot fight or destroy, can see intellectually this truth: In a war against death, it is by fighting and destroying the enemy that the value of life is affirmed.

In such a war, no living fighter need concern himself with pity for his enemy; this one twisted pain, at least, no one need feel.

But in any war the vital effect of pacifism is not on the foe, but on the pacifist.

I touched a peace-loving mind, very hungry for life. . . .

THE PEACEMAKER

CARR SWALLOWED A pain pill and tried to find a less uncomfortable position in the combat chair. He keyed his radio transmitter, and spoke:

"I come in peace. I have no weapons. I come to talk to you."

He waited. The cabin of his little one-man ship was silent. His radar screen showed the berserker machine still many light-seconds ahead of him. There was no reaction from it, but he knew that it had heard him.

Behind Carr was the Sol-type star he called sun, and his home planet, colonized from Earth a century before. It was a lonely settlement, out near the rim of the galaxy; until now, the berserker war had been no more than a remote horror in news stories. The colony's only real fighting ship had recently gone to join Karlsen's fleet in the defense of Earth, when the berserkers were said to be massing there. But now the enemy was here.

The people of Carr's planet were readying two more warships as fast as they could—they were a small colony, and not wealthy in resources. Even if the two ships could be made ready in time, they would hardly be a match for a berserker.

When Carr had taken his plan to the leaders of his planet, they had thought him mad. Go out and talk to it of peace and love? *Argue* with it? There might be some hope of converting the most depraved human to the cause of goodness and mercy, but what appeal could alter the built-in purpose of a machine?

"Why not talk to it of peace?" Carr had demanded. "Have you a better plan? I'm willing to go. I've nothing to lose."

They had looked at him, across the gulf that separates healthy planners from those who know they are dying. They knew his scheme would not work, but they could think of nothing that would. It would be at least ten days until the warships were ready. The little one-man ship was expendable, being unarmed. Armed, it would be no more than a provocation to a berserker. In the end, they let Carr take it, hoping there was a chance his arguments might delay the inevitable attack.

When Carr came within a million miles of the berserker, it stopped its own unhurried motion and seemed to wait for him, hanging in space in the orbital track of an airless planetoid, at a point from which the planetoid was still several days away.

"I am unarmed," he radioed again. "I come to talk with you, not to damage you. If those who built you were here, I would try to talk to them of peace and love. Do you understand?" He was serious about talking

61

love to the unknown builders; things like hatred and vengeance were not worth Carr's time now.

Suddenly it answered him: "Little ship, maintain your present speed and course toward me. Be ready to stop when ordered."

"I—I will." He had thought himself ready to face it, but he stuttered and shook at the mere sound of its voice. Now the weapons which could sterilize a planet would be trained on him alone. And there was worse than destruction to be feared, if one tenth of the stories about berserkers' prisoners were true. Carr did not let himself think about that.

When he was within ten thousand miles it ordered: "Stop. Wait where you are, relative to me."

Carr obeyed instantly. Soon he saw that it had launched toward him something about the size of his own ship—a little moving dot on his video screen, coming out of the vast fortress-shape that floated against the stars.

Even at this range he could see how scarred and battered that fortress was. He had heard that all of these ancient machines were damaged, from their long senseless campaign across the galaxy; but surely such apparent ruin as this must be exceptional.

The berserker's launch slowed and drew up beside his ship. Soon there came a clanging at the airlock.

"Open!" demanded the radio voice. "I must search you."

"Then will you listen to me?"

"Then I will listen."

He opened the lock, and stood aside for the half-dozen machines that entered. They looked not unlike robot valets and workers to Carr, except these were limping and worn, like their great master. Here and there a new part gleamed, but the machines' movements were often unsteady as they searched Carr, searched his cabin, probed everywhere on the little ship. When the search was completed one of the boarding machines had to be half-carried out by its fellows.

Another one of the machines, a thing with arms and hands like a man's, stayed behind. As soon as the airlock had closed behind the others, it settled itself in the combat chair and began to drive the ship toward the berserker.

"Wait!" Carr heard himself protesting. "I didn't mean I was surrendering!" The ridiculous words hung in the air, seeming to deserve no reply. Sudden panic made Carr move without thinking; he stepped forward and grabbed at the mechanical pilot, trying to pull it from the chair. It put one metal hand against his chest and shoved him across the cabin, so that he staggered and fell in the artificial gravity, thumping his head painfully against a bulkhead.

"In a matter of minutes we will talk about love and peace," said the radio.

Looking out through a port as his ship neared the immense berserker, Carr saw the scars of battle become plainer and plainer, even to his untaught eye. There were holes in the berserker's hull, there were square miles of bendings and swellings, and pits where the metal had once flowed molten. Rubbing his bumped head, Carr felt a faint thrill of pride. We've done that to it, he thought, we soft little living things. The martial feeling annoyed him in a way. He had always been something of a pacifist.

After some delay, a hatch opened in the berserker's side, and the ship followed the berserker's launch into darkness.

Now there was nothing to be seen through the port. Soon there came a gentle bump, as of docking. The mechanical pilot shut off the drive, and turned toward Carr and started to rise from its chair.

Something in it failed. Instead of rising smoothly, the pilot reared up, flailed for a moment with arms that sought a grip or balance, and then fell heavily to the deck. For half a minute it moved one arm, and made a grinding noise. Then it was still.

In the half minute of silence which followed, Carr realized that he was again master of his cabin; chance had given him that. If there was only something he could do—

"Leave your ship," said the berserker's calm voice. "There is an air-filled tube fitted to your airlock. It will lead you to a place where we can talk of peace and love."

Carr's eyes had focused on the engine switch, and then had looked beyond that, to the C-plus activator. In such proximity as this to a mass the size of the surrounding berserker, the C-plus effect was not a drive but a weapon—one of tremendous potential power.

Carr did not—or thought he did not—any longer fear sudden death. But now he found that with all his heart and soul he feared what might be prepared for him outside his airlock. All the horror stories came back. The thought of going out through that airlock now was unendurable. It was less terrifying for him to step carefully around the fallen pilot, to reach the controls and turn the engine back on.

"I can talk to you from here," he said, his voice quavering in spite of an effort to keep it steady.

After about ten seconds, the berserker said: "Your C-plus drive has safety devices. You will not be able to kamikaze me."

"You may be right," said Carr after a moment's thought. "But if a safety device does function, it might hurl my ship away from your center of mass, right through your hull. And your hull is in bad shape now, you don't want any more damage."

"You would die."

"I'll have to die sometime. But I didn't come out here to die, or to fight, but to talk to you, to try to reach some agreement."

"What kind of agreement?"

At last. Carr took a deep breath, and marshalled the arguments he had so often rehearsed. He kept his fingers resting gently on the C-plus activator, and his eyes alert on the instruments that normally monitored the hull for micrometeorite damage.

"I've had the feeling," he began, "that your attacks upon humanity may be only some ghastly mistake. Certainly we were not your original enemy."

"Life is my enemy. Life is evil." Pause. "Do you want to become goodlife?"

Carr closed his eyes for a moment; some of the horror stories were coming to life. But then he went firmly on with his argument. "From our point of view, it is you who are bad. We would like you to become a good machine, one that helps men instead of killing them. Is not building a higher purpose than destroying?"

There was a longer pause. "What evidence can you offer, that I should change my purpose?"

"For one thing, helping us will be a purpose easier of achievement. No one will damage you and oppose you."

"What is it to me, if I am damaged and opposed?"

Carr tried again. "Life is basically superior to non-life; and man is the highest form of life."

"What evidence do you offer?"

"Man has a spirit."

"I have learned that many men claim that. But do you not define this spirit as something beyond the perception of any machine? And are there not many men who deny that this spirit exists?"

"Spirit is so defined. And there are such men."

"Then I do not accept the argument of spirit."

Carr dug out a pain pill and swallowed it. "Still, you have no evidence that spirit does not exist. You must consider it as a possibility."

"That is correct."

"But leaving spirit out of the argument for now, consider the physical and chemical organization of life. Do you know anything of the delicacy and intricacy of organization in even a single living cell? And surely you must admit we humans carry wonderful computers inside our few cubic inches of skull."

"I have never had an intelligent captive to dissect," the mechanical voice informed him blandly. "Though I have received some relevant data from other machines. But you admit that your form is the determined result of the operation of physical and chemical laws?"

"Have *you* ever thought that those laws may have been designed to do just that—produce brains capable of intelligent action?"

There was a pause that stretched on and on. Carr's

throat felt dry and rough, as if he had been speaking for hours.

"I have never tried to use that hypothesis," it answered suddenly. "But if the construction of intelligent life is indeed so intricate, so dependent upon the laws of physics being as they are and not otherwise— then to serve life may be the highest purpose of a machine."

"You may be sure, our physical construction is intricate." Carr wasn't sure he could follow the machine's line of reasoning, but that hardly mattered if he could somehow win the game for life. He kept his fingers on the C-plus activator.

The berserker said: "If I am able to study some living cells—"

Like a hot iron on a nerve, the meteorite-damage indicator moved; something was at the hull. "Stop that!" he screamed, without thought. "The first thing you try, I'll kill you!"

Its voice was unevenly calm, as always. "There may have been some accidental contact with your hull. I am damaged and many of my commensal machines are unreliable. I mean to land on this approaching planetoid to mine for metal and repair myself as far as possible." The indicator was quiet again.

The berserker resumed its argument. "If I am able to study some living cells from an intelligent life-unit for a few hours, I expect I will find strong evidence for or against your claims. Will you provide me with cells?"

"You must have had prisoners, sometime." He said it as a suspicion; he really knew no reason why it must have had human captives. It could have learned the language from another berserker.

"No, I have never taken a prisoner."

It waited. The question it had asked still hung in the air.

"The only human cells on this ship are my own. Possibly I could give you a few of them."

"Half a cubic centimeter should be enough. Not a dangerous loss for you, I believe. I will not demand part of your brain. Also I understand that you wish to avoid the situation called pain. I am willing to help you avoid it, if possible."

Did it want to drug him? That seemed to simple. Always unpredictability, the stories said, and sometimes a subtlety out of hell.

He went on with the game. "I have all that is necessary. Be warned that my attention will hardly waver from my control panel. Soon I will place a tissue sample in the airlock for you."

He opened the ship's medical kit, took two pain-killers, and set very carefully to work with a sterile scalpel. He had had some biological training.

When the small wound was bandaged, he cleansed the tissue sample of blood and lymph and with unsteady fingers sealed it into a little tube. Without letting down his guard, he thought, for an instant, he dragged the fallen pilot to the airlock and left it there with the tissue sample. Utterly weary, he got back to the combat chair. When he switched the outer door open, he heard something come into the lock and leave again.

He took a pep pill. It would activate some pain, but he had to stay alert. Two hours passed. Carr forced himself to eat some emergency rations, watched the panel, and waited.

He gave a startled jump when the berserker spoke again; nearly six hours had gone by.

"You are free to leave," it was saying. "Tell the leading life-units of your planet that when I have refitted, I will be their ally. The study of your cells has convinced me that the human body is the highest creation of the universe, and that I should make it my purpose to help you. Do you understand?"

Carr felt numb. "Yes. Yes. I have convinced you. After you have refitted, you will fight on our side."

Something shoved hugely and gently at his hull. Through a port he saw stars, and he realized that the great hatch that had swallowed his ship was swinging open.

This far within the system, Carr necessarily kept his ship in normal space to travel. His last sight of the berserker showed it moving as if indeed about to let down upon the airless planetoid. Certainly it was not following him.

A couple of hours after being freed, he roused himself from contemplation of the radar screen, and went to spend a full minute considering the inner airlock door. At last he shook his head, dialed air into the lock, and entered it. The pilot-machine was gone, and the tissue sample. There was nothing out of the ordinary to be seen. Carr took a deep breath, as if relieved, closed up the lock again, and went to a port to spend some time watching the stars.

After a day he began to decelerate, so that when hours had added into another day, he was still a good distance from home. He ate, and slept, and watched his face in a mirror. He weighed himself, and watched the stars some more, with interest, like a man reexamining something long forgotten.

In two more days, gravity bent his course into a

hairpin ellipse around his home planet. With it bulking between him and the berserker's rock, Carr began to use his radio.

"Ho, on the ground, good news."

The answer came almost instantly. "We've been tracking you, Carr. What's going on? What's happened?"

He told them. "So that's the story up to now," he finished. "I expect the thing really needs to refit. Two warships attacking it now should win."

"Yes." There was excited talk in the background. Then the voice was back, sounding uneasy. "Carr— you haven't started a landing approach yet, so maybe you understand. The thing was probably lying to you."

"Oh, I know. Even that pilot-machine's collapse might have been staged. I guess the berserker was too badly shot up to want to risk a battle, so it tried another way. Must have sneaked the stuff into my cabin air, just before it let me go—or maybe left it in my airlock."

"What kind of stuff?"

"I'd guess it's some freshly mutated virus, designed for specific virulence against the tissue I gave it. It expected me to hurry home and land before getting sick, and spread a plague. It must have thought it was inventing biological warfare, using life against life, as we use machines to fight machines. But it needed that tissue sample to blood its pet viruses; it must have been telling the truth about never having a human prisoner."

"Some kind of virus, you think? What's it doing to you, Carr? Are you in pain? I mean, more than before?"

"No." Carr swiveled his chair to look at the little chart he had begun. It showed that in the last two days his weight loss had started to reverse itself. He looked down at his body, at the bandaged place near the center of a discolored inhuman-looking area. That area was smaller than it had been, and he saw a hint of new and healthy skin.

"What *is* the stuff doing to you?"

Carr allowed himself to smile, and to speak aloud his growing hope. "I think it's killing off my cancer."

For most men the war brought no miracles of healing, but a steady deforming pressure which seemed to have existed always, and which had no foreseeable end. Under this burden some men became like brutes, and the minds of others grew to be as terrible and implacable as the machines they fought against.

But I have touched a few rare human minds, the jewels of life, who rise to meet the greatest challenges by becoming surpremely men.

STONE PLACE

EARTH'S GOBI SPACEPORT was perhaps the biggest in all the small corner of the galaxy settled by Solarian man and his descendants; at least so thought Mitchell Spain, who had seen most of those ports in his twenty-four years of life.

But looking down now from the crowded, descending shuttle, he could see almost nothing of the Gobi's miles of ramp. The vast crowd below, meaning only joyful welcome, had defeated its own purpose by forcing back and breaking the police lines. Now the vertical string of descending shuttle-ships had to pause, searching for enough clear room to land.

Mitchell Spain, crowded into the lowest shuttle with a thousand other volunteers, was paying little attention to the landing problem for the moment. Into this jammed compartment, once a luxurious observation lounge, had just come Johann Karlsen himself; and this was Mitch's first chance for a good look at the newly appointed High Commander of Sol's defense, though Mitch had ridden Karlsen's spear-shaped flagship all the way from Austeel.

Karlsen was no older than Mitchell Spain, and no taller, his shortness somehow surprising at first glance. He had become ruler of the planet Austeel through the influence of his half-brother, the mighty Felipe Nogara, head of the empire of Esteel; but Karlsen held his position by his own talents.

"This field may be blocked for the rest of the day," Karlsen was saying now, to a cold-eyed Earthman who had just come aboard the shuttle from an aircar. "Let's have the ports open, I want to look around."

Glass and metal slid and reshaped themselves, and sealed ports became small balconies open to the air of Earth, the fresh smells of a living planet—open, also, to the roaring chant of the crowd a few hundred feet below: "Karlsen! Karlsen!"

As the High Commander stepped out onto a balcony to survey for himself the chances of landing, the throng of men in the lounge made a half-voluntary brief surging movement, as if to follow. These men were mostly Austeeler volunteers, with a sprinkling of adventurers like Mitchell Spain, the Martian wanderer who had signed up on Austeel for the battle bounty Karlsen offered.

"Don't crowd, outlander," said a tall man ahead of Mitch, turning and looking down at him.

"I answer to the name of Mitchell Spain." He let his voice rasp a shade deeper than usual. "No more an outlander here than you, I think."

The tall one, by his dress and accent, came from

Venus, a planet terraformed only within the last century, whose people were sensitive and proud in newness of independence and power. A Venerian might well be jumpy here, on a ship filled with men from a planet ruled by Felipe Nogara's brother.

"Spain—sounds like a Martian name," said the Venerian in a milder tone, looking down at Mitch.

Martians were not known for patience and long suffering. After another moment the tall one seemed to get tired of locking eyes and turned away.

The cold-eyed Earthman, whose face was somehow familiar to Mitch, was talking on the communicator, probably to the captain of the shuttle. "Drive on across the city, cross the Khosutu highway, and let down there."

Karlsen, back inside, said: "Tell him to go no more than about ten kilometers an hour; they seem to want to see me."

The statement was matter-of-fact; if people had made great efforts to see Johann Karlsen, it was only the courteous thing to greet them.

Mitch watched Karlsen's face, and then the back of his head, and the strong arms lifted to wave, as the High Commander stepped out again onto the little balcony. The crowd's roar doubled.

Is that all you feel, Karlsen, a wish to be courteous? Oh, no, my friend, you are acting. To be greeted with that thunder must do something vital to any man. It might exalt him; possibly it could disgust or frighten him, friendly as it was. You wear well your mask of courteous nobility, High Commander.

What was it like to be Johann Karlsen, come to save the world, when none of the really great and powerful ones seemed to care too much about it? With a bride of famed beauty to be yours when the battle had been won?

And what was brother Felipe doing today? Scheming, no doubt, to get economic power over yet another planet.

With another shift of the little mob inside the shuttle the tall Venerian moved from in front of Mitch, who could now see clearly out the port past Karlsen. Sea of faces, the old cliche, this was really it. How to write this . . . Mitch knew he would someday have to write it. If all men's foolishness was not permanently ended by the coming battle with the unliving, the battle bounty should suffice to let a man write for some time.

Ahead now were the bone-colored towers of Ulan Bator, rising beyond their fringe of suburban slideways and sunfields; and a highway; and bright multicolored pennants, worn by the aircars swarming out from the city in glad welcome. Now police aircars were keeping pace protectively with the spaceship, though there seemed to be no possible danger from anything but excess enthusiasm.

Another, special, aircar approached. The police craft touched it briefly and gently, then drew back with deference. Mitch stretched his neck, and made out a Carmpan insignia on the car. It was probably their ambassador to Sol, in person. The space shuttle eased to a dead slow creeping.

Some said that the Carmpan looked like machines themselves, but they were the strong allies of Earth-descended men in the war against the enemies of all life. If the Carmpan bodies were slow and squarish, their minds were visionary; if they were curiously unable to use force against any enemy, their indirect help was of great value.

Something near silence came over the vast crowd as the ambassador reared himself up in his open car; from his head and body, ganglions of wire and fiber stretched to make a hundred connections with Carmpan animals and equipment around him.

The crowd recognized the meaning of the network; a great sigh went up. In the shuttle, men jostled one another trying for a better view. The cold-eyed Earthman whispered rapidly into the communicator.

"Prophecy!" said a hoarse voice, near Mitch's ear.

"—of Probability!" came the ambassador's voice, suddenly amplified, seeming to pick up the thought in midphrase. The Carmpan Prophets of Probability were half mystics, half cold mathematicians. Karlsen's aides must have decided, or known, that this prophecy was going to be a favorable, inspiring thing which the crowd should hear, and had ordered the ambassador's voice picked up on a public address system.

"The hope, the living spark, to spread the flame of life!" The inhuman mouth chopped out the words, which still rose ringingly. The armlike appendages pointed straight to Karlsen, level on his balcony with the hovering aircar. "The dark metal thoughts are now of victory, the dead things make their plan to kill us all. But in this man before me now, there is life greater than any strength of metal. A power of life, to resonate—in all of us. I see, with Karlsen, victory—"

The strain on a Carmpan prophet in action was always immense, just as his accuracy was always high. Mitch had heard that the stresses involved were more topological than nervous or electrical. He had heard it, but like most Earth-descended, had never understood it.

"Victory," the ambassador repeated. "Victory . . . and then. . . ."

Something changed in the non-Solarian face. The cold-eyed Earthman was perhaps expert in reading alien expressions, or was perhaps just taking no chances. He whispered another command, and the amplification was taken from the Carmpan voice. A roar of approval mounted up past shuttle and aircar, from the great throng who thought the prophecy complete. But the ambassador had not finished, though now only those a few meters in front of him, inside the shuttle, could hear his faltering voice.

". . . then death, destruction, failure." The square body bent, but the alien eyes were still riveted on Karlsen. "He who wins everything . . . will die owning nothing. . . ."

The Carmpan bent down and his aircar moved away. In the lounge of the shuttle there was silence. The hurrahing outside sounded like mockery.

After long seconds, the High Commander turned in from the balcony and raised his voice: "Men, we who have heard the finish of the prophecy are few—but still we are many, to keep a secret. So I don't ask for secrecy. But spread the word, too, that I have no faith in prophecies that are not of God. The Carmpan have never claimed to be infallible."

The gloomy answer was unspoken, but almost telepathically loud among the group. Nine times out of ten, the Carmpan are right. There will be a victory, then death and failure.

But did the dark ending apply only to Johann Karlsen, or to the whole cause of the living? The men in the shuttle looked at one another, wondering and murmuring.

The shuttles found space to land, at the edge of Ulan Bator. Disembarking, the men found no chance for gloom, with a joyous crowd growing thicker by the moment around the ships. A lovely Earth girl came, wreathed in garlands, to throw a flowery loop around Mitchell Spain, and to kiss him. He was an ugly man, quite unused to such willing attentions.

Still, he noticed when the High Commander's eye fell on him.

"You, Martian, come with me to the General Staff meeting. I want to show a representative group in there so they'll know I'm not just my brother's agent. I need one or two who were born in Sol's light."

"Yes, sir." Was there no other reason why Karlsen had singled him out? They stood together in the crowd, two short men looking levelly at each other. One ugly and flower-bedecked, his arm still around a girl who stared with sudden awed recognition at the other man, who was magnetic in a way beyond handsomeness or ugliness. The ruler of a planet, perhaps to be the savior of all life.

"I like the way you keep people from standing on your toes in a crowd," said Karlsen to Mitchell Spain. "Without raising your voice or uttering threats. What's your name and rank?"

Military organization tended to be vague, in this war where everything that lived was on the same side. "Mitchell Spain, sir. No rank assigned, yet. I've been training with the marines. I was on Austeel when you offered a good battle bounty, so here I am."

"Not to defend Mars?"

"I suppose, that too. But I might as well get paid for it."

Karlsen's high-ranking aides were wrangling and shouting now, about groundcar transportation to the staff meeting. This seemed to leave Karlsen with time to talk. He thought, and recognition flickered on his face.

"Mitchell Spain? The poet?"

"I—I've had a couple of things published. Nothing much. . . ."

"Have you combat experience?"

"Yes, I was aboard one berserker, before it was pacified. That was out—"

"Later, we'll talk. Probably have some marine command for you. Experienced men are scarce. Hemphill, where *are* those groundcars?"

The cold-eyed Earthman turned to answer. Of course his face had been familiar; this was Hemphill, fanatic hero of a dozen berserker fights. Mitch was faintly awed, in spite of himself.

At last the groundcars came. The ride was into Ulan Bator. The military center would be under the metropolis, taking full advantage of the defensive force fields that could be extended up into space to protect the area of the city.

Riding down the long elevator zigzag to the buried War Room, Mitch found himself again next to Karlsen.

"Congratulations on your coming marriage, sir." Mitch didn't know if he liked Karlsen or not; but already he felt curiously certain of him, as if he had known the man for years. Karlsen would know he was not trying to curry favor.

The High Commander nodded. "Thank you." He

hesitated for a moment, then produced a small photo. In an illusion of three dimensions it showed the head of a young woman, golden hair done in the style favored by the new aristocracy of Venus.

There was no need for any polite stretching of truth. "She's very beautiful."

"Yes." Karlsen looked long at the picture, as if reluctant to put it away. "There are those who say this will be only a political alliance. God knows we need one. But believe me, Poet, she means far more than that to me."

Karlsen blinked suddenly and, as if amused at himself, gave Mitch a why-am-I-telling-you-all-this look. The elevator floor pressed up under the passengers' feet, and the doors sighed open. They had reached the catacomb of the General Staff.

Many of the staff, though not an absolute majority, were Venerian in these days. From their greeting it was plain that the Venerian members were coldly hostile to Nogara's brother.

Humanity was, as always, a tangle of cliques and alliances. The brains of the Solarian Parliment and the Executive had been taxed to find a High Commander. If some objected to Johann Karlsen, no one who knew him had any honest doubt of his ability. He brought with him to battle many trained men, and unlike some mightier leaders, he had been willing to take responsibility for the defense of Sol.

In the frigid atmosphere in which the staff meeting opened, there was nothing to do but get quickly to business. The enemy, the berserker machines, had abandoned their old tactics of single, unpredictable raids—for slowly over the last decades the defenses of life had been strengthened.

There were now thought to be about two hundred berserkers; to meet humanity's new defenses they had recently formed themselves into a fleet, with concentrated power capable of overwhelming one at a time all centers of human resistance. Two strongly defended planets had already been destroyed. A massed human fleet was needed, first to defend Sol, and then to meet and break the power of the unliving.

"So far, then, we are agreed," said Karlsen, straightening up from the plotting table and looking around at the General Staff. "We have not as many ships or as many trained men as we would like. Perhaps no government away from Sol has contributed all it could."

Kemal, the Venerian admiral, glanced around at his planetmen, but declined the chance to comment on the weak contribution of Karlsen's own half-brother, Nogara. There was no living being upon whom Earth, Mars, and Venus could really agree, as the leader for this war. Kemal seemed to be willing to try and live with Nogara's brother.

Karlsen went on: "We have available for combat two hundred and forty-three ships, specially constructed or modified to suit the new tactics I propose to use. We are all grateful for the magnificent Venerian contribution of a hundred ships. Six of them, as you probably all know, mount the new long-range C-plus cannon."

The praise produced no visible thaw among the Venerians. Karlsen went on: "We seem to have a numerical advantage of about forty ships. I needn't tell you how the enemy outgun and outpower us, unit for unit.'' He paused. ''The ram-and-board tactics should give us just the element of surprise we need.''

Perhaps the High Commander was choosing his words carefully, not wanting to say that some element of surprise offered the only logical hope of success. After the decades-long dawning of hope, it would be too much to say that. Too much for even these tough-minded men who knew how a berserker machine weighed in the scales of war against any ordinary warship.

''One big problem is trained men,'' Karlsen continued, ''to lead the boarding parties. I've done the best I can, recruiting. Of those ready and in training as boarding marines now, the bulk are Esteelers.''

Admiral Kemal seemed to guess what was coming; he started to push back his chair and rise, then waited, evidently wanting to make certain.

Karlsen went on in the same level tone. ''These trained marines will be formed into companies, and one company assigned to each warship. Then—''

''One moment, High Commander Karlsen.'' Kemal had risen.

''Yes?''

''Do I understand that you mean to station companies of Esteelers aboard Venerian ships?''

''In many cases my plan will mean that, yes. You protest?''

''I do.'' The Venerian looked around at his planet-men. ''We all do.''

''Nevertheless it is so ordered.''

Kemal looked briefly around at his fellows once more, then sat down, blankfaced. The stenocameras in the room's corners emitted their low sibilance, reminding all that the proceedings were being recorded.

A vertical crease appeared briefly in the High Commander's forehead, and he looked for long thoughtful seconds at the Venerians before resuming his talk. But what else was there to do, except put Esteelers onto Venerian ships?

They won't let you be a hero, Karlsen, thought Mitchell Spain. The universe is bad; and men are fools, never really all on the same side in any war.

In the hold of the Venerian warship *Solar Spot* the armor lay packed inside a padded coffinlike crate. Mitch knelt beside it inspecting the knee and elbow joints.

"Want me to paint some insignia on it, Captain?"

The speaker was a young Esteeler named Fishman, one of the newly formed marine company Mitch now commanded. Fishman had picked up a multicolor paintstick somewhere, and he pointed with it to the suit.

Mitch glanced around the hold, which was swarming with his men busily opening crates of equipment. He had decided to let things run themselves as much as possible.

"Insignia? Why, I don't think so. Unless you have some idea for a company insignia. That might be a good thing to have."

There seemed no need for any distinguishing mark on his armored suit. It was of Martian make, distinctive in style, old but with the latest improvements built in—probably no man wore better. The barrel chest already bore one design—a large black spot shattered by jagged red—showing that Mitch had been in at the "death" of one berserker. Mitch's uncle had worn the same armor; the men of Mars had always gone in great numbers out into space.

"Sergeant McKendrick," Mitch asked, "what do you think about having a company insignia?"

The newly appointed sergeant, an intelligent-looking young man, paused in walking past, and looked from Mitch to Fishman as if trying to decide who stood where on insignia before committing himself. Then he looked between them, his expression hardening.

A thin-faced Venerian, evidently an officer, had entered the hold with a squad of six men behind him, armbanded and sidearmed. Ship's Police.

The officer took a few steps and then stood motionless, looking at the paintstick in Fishman's hand. When everyone in the hold was silently watching him, he asked quietly:

"Why have you stolen from ships' stores?"

"Stolen—*this*?" The young Esteeler held up the paintstick, half-smiling, as if ready to share a joke.

They didn't come joking with a police squad, or, if they did, it was not the kind of joke a Martian appreciated. Mitch still knelt beside his crated armor. There was an unloaded carbine inside the suit's torso and he put his hand on it.

"We are at war, and we are in space," the thin-faced officer went on, still speaking mildly, standing relaxed, looking round at the open-mouthed Esteeler company. "Everyone aboard a Venerian ship is subject to law. For stealing from the ship's stores, while we face the enemy, the penalty is death. By hanging. Take him away." He made an economical gesture to his squad.

The paintstick clattered loudly on the deck. Fishman looked as if he might be going to topple over, half the smile still on his face.

Mitch stood up, the carbine in the crook of his arm. It was a stubby weapon with heavy double barrel, really a miniature recoilless cannon, to be used in free fall to destroy armored machinery. "Just a minute," Mitch said.

A couple of the police squad had begun to move uncertainly toward Fishman. They stopped at once, as if glad of an excuse for doing so.

The officer looked at Mitch, and raised one cool eyebrow. "Do you know what the penalty is, for threatening me?"

"Can't be any worse than the penalty for blowing your ugly head off. I'm Captain Mitchell Spain, marine company commander on this ship, and nobody just comes in here and drags my men away and hangs them. Who are you?"

"I am Mr. Salvador," said the Venerian. His eyes appraised Mitch, no doubt establishing that he was Martian. Wheels were turning in Mr. Salvador's calm brain, and plans were changing. He said: "Had I known that a *man* commanded this . . . group . . . I would not have thought an object lesson necessary. Come." This last word was addressed to his squad and accompanied by another simple elegant gesture. The six lost no time, preceding him to the exit. Salvador's eyes motioned Mitch to follow him to the door. After a moment's hesitation Mitch did so, while Salvador waited for him, still unruffled.

"Your men will follow you eagerly now, Captain Spain," he said in a voice too low for anyone else to hear. "And the time will come when you will willingly follow me." With a faint smile, as if of appreciation, he was gone.

There was a moment of silence; Mitch stared at the closed door, wondering. Then a roar of jubilation burst out and his back was being pounded.

When most of the uproar had died down, one of the men asked him: "Captain—what'd he mean, calling himself Mister?"

"To the Venerians, it's some kind of political rank. You guys look here! I may need some honest witnesses." Mitch held up the carbine for all to see, and broke open the chambers and clips, showing it to be unloaded. There was renewed excitement, more howls and jokes at the expense of the retreated Venerians.

But Salvador had not thought himself defeated.

"McKendrick, call the bridge. Tell the ship's captain I want to see him. The rest of you men, let's get on with this unpacking."

Young Fishman, paintstick in hand again, stood staring vacantly downward as if contemplating a design for the deck. It was beginning to soak in, how close a thing it had been.

An object lesson?

The ship's captain was coldly taciturn with Mitch, but he indicated there were no present plans for hanging any Esteelers on the *Solar Spot*. During the next sleep period Mitch kept armed sentries posted in the marines' quarters.

The next day he was summoned to the flagship. From the launch he had a view of a dance of bright dots, glinting in the light of distant Sol. Part of the fleet was already at ramming practice.

Behind the High Commander's desk sat neither a

poetry critic nor a musing bridegroom, but the ruler of a planet.

"Captain Spain—sit down."

To be given a chair seemed a good sign. Waiting for Karlsen to finish some paperwork, Mitch's thoughts wandered, recalling customs he had read about, ceremonies of saluting and posturing men had used in the past when huge permanent organizations had been formed for the sole purpose of killing other men and destroying their property. Certainly men were still as greedy as ever; and now the berserker war was accustoming them again to mass destruction. Could those old days, when life fought all-out war against life, ever come again?

With a sigh, Karlsen pushed aside his papers. "What happened yesterday, between you and Mr. Salvador?"

"He said he meant to hang one of my men." Mitch gave the story, as simply as he could. He omitted only Salvador's parting words, without fully reasoning out why he did. "When I'm made responsible for men," he finished, "nobody just walks in and hangs them. Though I'm not fully convinced they would have gone that far, I meant to be as serious about it as they were."

The High Commander picked out a paper from his desk litter. "Two Esteeler marines have been hanged already. For fighting."

"Damned arrogant Venerians I'd say."

"I want none of that, Captain!"

"Yes, sir. But I'm telling you we came mighty close to a shooting war, yesterday on the *Solar Spot*."

"I realize that." Karlsen made a gesture expressive of futility. "Spain, is it impossible for the people of this fleet to cooperate, even when the survival of—what is it?"

The Earthman, Hemphill, had entered the cabin without ceremony. His thin lips were pressed tighter than ever. "A courier has just arrived with news. Atsog is attacked."

Karlsen's strong hand crumpled papers with an involuntary twitch. "Any details?"

"The courier captain says he thinks the whole berserker fleet was there. The ground defenses were still resisting strongly when he pulled out. He just got his ship away in time.

Atsog—a planet closer to Sol than the enemy had been thought to be. It was Sol they were coming for, all right. They must know it was the human center.

More people were at the cabin door. Hemphill stepped aside for the Venerian, Admiral Kemal. Mr. Salvador, hardly glancing at Mitch, followed the admiral in.

"You have heard the news, High Commander?" Salvador began. Kemal, just ready to speak himself, gave his political officer an annoyed glance, but said nothing.

"That Atsog is attacked, yes," said Karlsen.

"My ships can be ready to move in two hours," said Kemal.

Karlsen sighed, and shook his head. "I watched today's maneuvers. The fleet can hardly be ready in two weeks."

Kemal's shock and rage seemed genuine. "You'd do that? You'd let a Venerian planet die just because we haven't knuckled under to your brother? Because we discipline his damned Esteeler—"

"Admiral Kemal, you will control yourself! You, and everyone else, are subject to discipline while I command!"

Kemal got himself in hand, apparently with great effort.

Karlsen's voice was not very loud, but the cabin seemed to resonate with it.

"You call hangings part of your discipline. I swear by the name of God that I will use every hanging, if I must, to enforce some kind of unity in this fleet. Understand, this fleet is the only military power that can oppose the massed berserkers. Trained, and unified, we can destroy them."

No listener could doubt it, for the moment.

"But whether Atsog falls, or Venus, or Esteel, I will not risk this fleet until I judge it ready."

Into the silence, Salvador said, with an air of respect: "High Commander, the courier reported one thing more. That the Lady Christina de Dulcin was visiting on Atsog when the attack began—and that she must be there still."

Karlsen closed his eyes for two seconds. Then he looked round at all of them. "If you have no further military business, gentlemen, get out." His voice was still steady.

Walking beside Mitch down the flagship corridor, Hemphill broke a silence to say thoughtfully: "Karlsen is the man the cause needs, now. Some Venerians have approached me, tentatively, about joining a plot—I refused. We must make sure that Karlsen remains in command."

"A plot?"

Hemphill did not elaborate.

Mitch said: "What they did just now was pretty low—letting him make that speech about going slow, no matter what—and then breaking the news to him about his lady being on Atsog."

Hemphill said: "He knew already she was there.

That news arrived on yesterday's courier."

There was a dark nebula, made up of clustered billions of rocks and older than the sun, named the Stone Place by men. Those who gathered there now were not men and they gave nothing a name; they hoped nothing, feared nothing, wondered at nothing. They had no pride and no regret, but they had plans—a billion subtleties, carved from electircal pressure and flow—and their built-in purpose, toward which their planning circuits moved. As if by instinct the berserker machines had formed themselves into a fleet when the time was ripe, when the eternal enemy, Life, had begun to mass its strength.

The planet named Atsog in the life-language had yielded a number of still-functioning life-units from its deepest shelters, though millions had been destroyed while their stubborn defenses were beaten down. Functional life-units were sources of valuable information. The mere threat of certain stimuli usually brought at least limited cooperation from any life-unit.

The life-unit (designating itself General Bradin) which had controlled the defense of Atsog was among those captured almost undamaged. Its dissection was begun within perception of the other captured life-units. The thin outer covering tissue was delicately removed, and placed upon a suitable form to preserve it for further study. The life-units which controlled others were examined carefully, whenever possible.

After this stimulus, it was no longer possible to communicate intelligibly with General Bradin; in a matter of hours it ceased to function at all.

In itself a trifling victory, the freeing of this small unit of watery matter from the aberration called Life.

But the flow of information now increased from the nearby units which had perceived the process.

It was soon confirmed that the life-units were assembling a fleet. More detailed information was sought. One important line of questioning concerned the life-unit which would control this fleet. Gradually, from interrogations and the reading of captured records, a picture emerged.

A name: Johann Karlsen. A biography. Contradictory things were said about him, but the facts showed he had risen rapidly to a position of control over millions of life-units.

Throughout the long war, the berserker computers had gathered and collated all available data on the men who became leaders of Life. Now against this data they matched, point for point, every detail that could be learned about Johann Karlsen.

The behavior of these leading units often resisted analysis, as if some quality of the life-disease in them was forever beyond the reach of machines. These individuals used logic, but sometimes it seemed they were not bound by logic. The most dangerous life-units of all sometimes acted in ways that seemed to contradict the known supremacy of the laws of physics and chance, as if they could be minds possessed of true free will, instead of its illusion.

And Karlsen was one of these, supremely one of these. His fitting of the dangerous pattern became plainer with every new comparison.

In the past, such life-units had been troublesome local problems. For one of them to command the whole life-fleet with a decisive battle approaching, was extremely dangerous to the cause of Death.

The outcome of the approaching battle seemed almost certain to be favorable, since there were probably only two hundred ships in the life-fleet. But the brooding berserkers could not be certain enough of anything, while a unit like Johann Karlsen led the living. And if the battle was long postponed the enemy Life could become stronger. There were hints that inventive Life was developing new weapons, newer and more powerful ships.

The wordless conference reached a decision. There were berserker reserves, which had waited for millennia along the galactic rim, dead and uncaring in their hiding places among dust clouds and heavy nebulae, and on dark stars. For this climactic battle they must be summoned, the power of Life to resist must be broken now.

From the berserker fleet at the Stone Place, between Atsog's Sun and Sol, courier machines sped out toward the galactic rim.

It would take some time for all the reserves to gather. Meanwhile, the interrogations went on.

"Listen, I've decided to help you, see. About this guy Karlsen, I know you want to find out about him. Only I got a delicate brain. If anything hurts me, my brain don't work at all, so no rough stuff on me, understand? I'll be no good to you ever if you use rough stuff on me."

This prisoner was unusual. The interrogating computer borrowed new circuits for itself, chose symbols and hurled them back at the life-unit.

"What can you tell me about Karlsen?"

"Listen you're gonna treat me right, aren't you?"

"Useful information will be rewarded. Untruth will bring you unpleasant stimuli."

"I'll tell you this now—the woman Karlsen was going to marry is here. You caught her alive in the same shelter General Bradin was in. Now, if you sort of give me control over some other prisoners, make things nice for me, why I bet I can think up the best way for you to use her. If you just tell him you've got her, why he might not believe you, see?"

Out on the galactic rim, the signals of the giant heralds called out the hidden reserves of the unliving. Subtle detectors heard the signals, and triggered the great engines into cold flame. The force field brain in each strategic housing awoke to livelier death. Each reserve machine began to move, with metallic leisure shaking loose its cubic miles of weight and power freeing itself from dust, or ice, or age-old mud, or solid rock—then rising and turning, orienting itself in space. All converging, they drove faster than light toward the Stone Place, where the destroyers of Atsog awaited their reinforcement.

With the arrival of each reserve machine, the linked berserker computers saw victory more probable. But still the quality of one life-unit made all of their computations uncertain.

Felipe Nogara raised a strong and hairy hand, and wiped it gently across one glowing segment of the panel before his chair. The center of his private study was filled by an enormous display sphere, which now showed a representation of the explored part of the galaxy. At Nogara's gesture the sphere dimmed, then began to relight itself in a slow intricate sequence.

A wave of his hand had just theoretically eliminated the berserker fleet as a factor in the power game. To leave it in, he told himself, diffused the probabilities too widely. It was really the competing power of Venus—and that of two or three other prosperous, aggressive planets—which occupied his mind.

Well insulated in this private room from the hum of Esteel City and from the routine press of business, Nogara watched his computers' new prediction take shape, showing the political power structure as it might exist one year from now, two years, five. As he had expected, this sequence showed Esteel expanding in influence. It was even possible that he could become ruler of the human galaxy.

Nogara wondered at his own calm in the face of such an idea. Twelve or fifteen years ago he had driven with all his power of intellect and will to advance himself. Gradually, the moves in the game had come to seem automatic. Today, there was a chance that almost every thinking being known to exist would come to acknowledge him as ruler—and it meant less to him than the first local election he had ever won.

Diminishing returns, of course. The more gained, the greater gain needed to produce an equal pleasure. At least when he was alone. If his aides were watching this prediction now it would certainly excite them, and he would catch their excitement.

But, being alone, he sighed. The berserker fleet would not vanish at the wave of a hand. Today, what was probably the final plea for more help had arrived from Earth. The trouble was that granting Sol more help would take ships and men and money from Nogara's expansion projects. Wherever he did that now, he stood to loose out, eventually, to other men. Old Sol would have to survive the coming attack with no more help from Esteel.

Nogara realized, wondering dully at himself, that he would as soon see even Esteel destroyed as see control slip from his hands. Now why? He could not say he loved his planet or his people, but he had been, by and large, a good ruler, not a tyrant. Good government was, after all, good politics.

His desk chimed the melodious notes that meant something was newly available for his amusement. Nogara chose to answer.

"Sir," said a woman's voice, "two new possibilities are in the shower room now."

Projected from hidden cameras, a scene glowed into life above Nogara's desk—bodies gleaming in a spray of water.

"They are from prison, sir, anxious for any reprieve."

Watching, Nogara felt only a weariness; and, yes, something like self-contempt. He questioned himself: Where in all the universe is there a reason why I should not seek pleasure as I choose? And again: Will I dabble in sadism, next? And if I do, what of it?

But what after that?

Having paused respectfully, the voice asked: "Perhaps this evening you would prefer something different?"

"Later," he said. The scene vanished. Maybe I should try to be a Believer for a while, he thought. What an intense thrill it must be for Johann to sin. If he ever does.

That had been a genuine pleasure, seeing Johann given command of the Solarian fleet, watching the Venerians boil. But it had raised another problem.

Johann, victorious over the berserkers, would emerge as the greatest hero in human history. Would that not make even Johann dangerously ambitious? The thing to do would be to ease him out of the public eye, give him some high-ranked job, honest, but dirty and inglorious. Hunting out outlaws somewhere. Johann would probably accept that, being Johann. But if Johann bid for galactic power, he would have to take his chances. Any pawn on the board might be removed.

Nogara shook his head. Suppose Johann lost the coming battle, and lost Sol? A berserker victory would not be a matter of diffusing probabilities, that was pleasant doubletalk for a tired mind to fool itself with. A berserker victory would mean the end of Earthman in the galaxy, probably within a few years. No computer was needed to see that.

There was a little bottle in his desk; Nogara brought it out and looked at it. The end of the chess game was in it, the end of all pleasure and boredom and pain. Looking at the vial caused him no emotion. In it was a powerful drug which threw a man into a kind of ecstasy—a transcendental excitement that within a few minutes burst the heart or the blood vessels of the brain. Someday, when all else was exhausted, when it was completely a berserker universe . . .

He put the vial away, and he put away the final appeal from Earth. What did it all matter? Was it not a berserker universe already, everything determined by the random swirls of condensing gas, before the stars were born?

Felipe Nogara leaned back in his chair, watching his computers marking out the galactic chessboard.

Through the fleet the rumor spread that Karlsen

delayed because it was a Venerian colony under siege. Aboard the *Solar Spot*, Mitch saw no delays for any reason. He had time for only work, quick meals, and sleep. When the final ram-and-board drill had been completed, the last stores and ammunition loaded, Mitch was too tired to feel much except relief. He rested, not frightened or elated, while the *Spot* wheeled into a rank with forty other arrow-shaped ships, dipped with them into the first C-plus jump of the deep space search, and began to hunt the enemy.

It was days later before dull routine was broken by a jangling battle alarm. Mitch was awakened by it; before his eyes were fully opened, he was scrambling into the armored suit stored under his bunk. Nearby, some marines grumbled about practice alerts; but none of them was moving slowly.

"This is High Commander Karlsen speaking," boomed the overhead speakers. "This is not a practice alert; repeat, not practice. Two berserkers have been sighted. One we've just glimpsed at extreme range. Likely it will get away, though the Ninth Squadron is chasing it.

"The other is not going to escape. In a matter of minutes we will have it englobed, in normal space. We are not going to destroy it by bombardment; we are going to soften it up a bit, and then see how well we can really ram and board. If there are any bugs left in our tactics, we'd better find out now. Squadrons Two, Four, and Seven will each send one ship to the ramming attack. I'm going back on Command Channel now, Squadron Commanders."

"Squadron Four," sighed Sergeant McKendrick. "More Esteelers in our company than any other. How can we miss?"

The marines lay like dragon's teeth seeded in the dark, strapped into the padded acceleration couches that had been their bunks, while the psych-music tried to lull them, and those who were Believers prayed. In the darkness Mitch listened on intercom, and passed on to his men the terse battle reports that came to him as marine commander on the ship.

He was afraid. What was death, that men should fear it so? It could only be the end of all experience. That end was inevitable, and beyond imagination, and he feared it.

The preliminary bombardment did not take long. Two hundred and thirty ships of life held a single trapped enemy in the center of their hollow sphere formation. Listening in the dark to laconic voices, Mitch heard how the berserker fought back, as if with the finest human courage and contempt for odds. Could you really fight machines, when you could never make them suffer pain or fear?

But you could defeat machines. And this time, for once, humanity had far too many guns. It would be easy to blow this berserker into vapor. Would it be best to do so? There were bound to be marine casualties in any boarding, no matter how favorable the odds. But a true combat test of the boarding scheme was badly needed before the decisive battle came to be fought. And, too, this enemy might hold living prisoners who might be rescued by boarders. A High Commander did well to have a rocklike certainty of his own rightness.

The order was given. The *Spot* and two other chosen ships fell in toward the battered enemy at the center of the englobement.

Straps held Mitch firmly, but the gravity had been turned off for the ramming, and weightlessness gave the impression that his body would fly and vibrate like a pellet shaken in a bottle with the coming impact. Soundless dark, soft cushioning, and lulling music; but a few words came into the helmet and the body cringed, knowing that outside were the black cold guns and the hurtling machines, unimaginable forces leaping now to meet. Now—

Reality shattered in through all the protection and the padding. The shaped atomic charge at the tip of the ramming prow opened the berserker's skin. In five seconds of crashing impact, the prow vaporized, melted, and crumpled its length away, the true hull driving behind it until the *Solar Spot* was sunk like an arrow into the body of the enemy.

Mitch spoke for the last time to the bridge of the *Solar Spot,* while his men lurched past him in free fall, their suit lights glaring.

"My panel shows Sally Port Three the only one not blocked," he said. "We're all going out that way."

"Remember," said a Venerian voice. "Your first job is to protect this ship against counterattack."

"Roger." If they wanted to give him offensively unnecessary reminders, now was not the time for argument. He broke contact with the bridge and hurried after his men.

The other two ships were to send their boarders fighting toward the strategic housing, somewhere deep in the berserker's center. The marines from the *Solar Spot* were to try to find and save any prisoners the berserker might hold. A berserker usually held prisoners near its surface, so the first search would be made by squads spreading out under the hundreds of square kilometers of hull.

In the dark chaos of wrecked machinery just outside

the sally port there was no sign yet of counterattack. The berserkers had supposedly not been built to fight battles inside their own metallic skins—on this rested the fleet's hopes for success in a major battle.

Mitch left forty men to defend the hull of the *Spot*, and himself led a squad of ten out into the labyrinth. There was no use setting himself up in a command post—communications in here would be impossible, once out of line-of-sight.

The first man in each searching squad carried a mass spectrometer, an instrument that would detect the stray atoms of oxygen bound to leak from compartments where living beings breathed. The last man wore on one hand a device to blaze a trail with arrows of luminous paint; without a trail, getting lost in this three-dimensional maze would be almost inevitable.

"Got a scent, Captain," said Mitch's spectrometer man, after five minutes' casting through the squad's assigned sector of the dying berserker.

"Keep on it." Mitch was second in line, his carbine ready.

The detector man led the way through a dark and weightless mechanical universe. Several times he paused to adjust his instrument and wave its probe. Otherwise the pace was rapid; men trained in free fall, and given plenty of holds to thrust and steer by, could move faster than runners.

A towering, multijointed shape rose up before the detector man, brandishing blue-white welding arcs like swords. Before Mitch was aware of aiming, his carbine fired twice. The shells ripped the machine open and pounded it backward; it was only some semirobotic maintenance device, not built for fighting.

The detector man had nerve; he plunged straight on.

The squad kept pace with him, their suit lights scouting out unfamiliar shapes and distances, cutting knife-edge shadows in the vacuum, glare and darkness mellowed only by reflection.

"Getting close!"

And then they came to it. It was a place like the top of a huge dry well. An ovoid like a ship's launch, very thickly armored, had apparently been raised through the well from deep inside the berserker, and now clamped to a dock.

"It's the launch, it's oozing oxygen."

"Captain, there's some kind of airlock on this side. Outer door's open."

It looked like the smooth and easy entrance of a trap.

"Keep your eyes open." Mitch went into the airlock. "Be ready to blast me out of here if I don't show in one minute."

It was an ordinary airlock, probably cut from some human spaceship. He shut himself inside, and then got the inner door open.

Most of the interior was a single compartment. In the center was an acceleration couch, holding a nude female mannikin. He drifted near, saw that her head had been depilated and that there were tiny beads of blood still on her scalp, as if probes had just been withdrawn.

When his suit lamp hit her face she opened dead blue staring eyes, blinking mechanically. Still not sure that he was looking at a living human being, Mitch drifted beside her and touched her arm with metal fingers. Then all at once her face became human, her eyes coming from death through nightmare to reality. She saw him and cried out. Before he could free her there were crystal drops of tears in the weightless air.

Listening to his rapid orders, she held one hand modestly in front of her, and the other over her raw scalp. Then she nodded, and took into her mouth the end of a breathing tube that would dole air from Mitch's suit tank. In a few more seconds he had her wrapped in a clinging, binding rescue blanket, temporary proof against vacuum and freezing.

The detector man had found no oxygen source except the launch. Mitch ordered his squad back along their luminous trail.

At the sally port, he heard that things were not going well with the attack. Real fighting robots were defending the strategic housing; at least eight men had been killed down there. Two more ships were going to ram and board.

Mitch carried the girl through the sally port and three more friendly hatches. The monstrously thick hull of the ship shuddered and sang around him; the *Solar Spot*, her mission accomplished, boarders retrieved, was being withdrawn. Full weight came back, and light.

"In here, Captain."

QUARANTINE, said the sign. A berserker's prisoner might have been deliberately infected with something contagious; men now knew how to deal with such tricks.

Inside the infirmary he set her down. While medics and nurses scrambled around, he unfolded the blanket from the girl's face, remembering to leave it curled over her shaven head, and opened his own helmet.

"You can spit out the tube now," he told her, in his rasping voice.

She did so, and opened her eyes again.

"Oh, are you real?" she whispered. Her hand pushed its way out of the blanket folds and slid over his armor. "Oh, let me touch a human being again!" Her hand moved up to his exposed face and gripped his cheek and neck.

"I'm real enough. You're all right now."

One of the bustling doctors came to a sudden, frozen halt, staring at the girl. Then he spun around on his heel and hurried away. What was wrong?

Others sounded confident, reassuring the girl as they ministered to her. She wouldn't let go of Mitch, she became nearly hysterical when they tried gently to separate her from him.

"I guess you'd better stay," a doctor told him.

He sat there holding her hand, his helmet and gauntlets off. He looked away while they did medical things to her. They still spoke easily; he thought they were finding nothing much wrong.

"What's your name?" she asked him when the medics were through for the moment. Her head was bandaged; her slender arm came from beneath the sheets to maintain contact with his hand.

"Mitchell Spain." Now that he got a good look at her, a living young human female, he was in no hurry at all to get away. "What's yours?"

A shadow crossed her face. "I'm—not sure."

There was a sudden commotion at the infirmary door; High Commander Karlsen was pushing past protesting doctors into the QUARANTINE area. Karlsen came on until he was standing beside Mitch, but he was not looking at Mitch.

"Chris," he said to the girl. "Thank God." There were tears in his eyes.

The Lady Christina de Dulcin turned her eyes from Mitch to Johann Karlsen, and screamed in abject terror.

"Now, Captain. Tell me how you found her and brought her out."

Mitch began his tale. The two men were alone in Karlsen's monastic cabin, just off the flagship's bridge. The fight was over, the berserker a torn and harmless hulk. No other prisoners had been aboard it.

"They planned to send her back to me," Karlsen said, staring into space, when Mitch had finished his account. "We attacked before it could launch her toward us. It kept her out of the fighting, and sent her back to me."

Mitch was silent.

Karlsen's red-rimmed eyes fastened on him. "She's been brainwashed, Poet. It can be done with some permanence, you know, when advantage is taken of the subject's natural tendencies. I suppose she's never thought too much of me. There were political reasons for her to consent to our marriage . . . she screams when the doctors even mention my name. They tell me it's possible that horrible things were done to her by some man-shaped machine made to look like me. Other people are tolerable, to a degree. But it's you she wants to be alone with, you she needs."

"She cried out when I left her, but—me?"

"The natural tendency, you see. For her to . . . love . . . the man who saved her. The machines set her mind to fasten all the joy of rescue upon the first male human face she saw. The doctors assure me such things can be done. They've given her drugs, but even in sleep the instruments show her nightmares, her pain, and she cries out for you. What do you feel toward her?"

"Sir, I'll do anything I can. What do you want of me?"

"I want you to stop her suffering, what else?" Karlsen's voice rose to a ragged shout. "Stay alone with her, stop her pain if you can!"

He got himself under a kind of control. "Go on. The doctors will take you in. Your gear will be brought over from the *Solar Spot.*"

Mitch stood up. Any words he could think of sounded in his mind like sickening attempts at humor. He nodded, and hurried out.

"This is your last chance to join us," said the Venerian, Salvador, looking up and down the dim corridors of this remote outer part of the flagship. "Our patience is worn, and we will strike soon. With the De Dulcin woman in her present condition, Nogara's brother is doubly unfit to command."

The Venerian must be carrying a pocket spy-jammer; a multisonic whine was setting Hemphill's teeth on edge. And so was the Venerian.

"Karlsen is vital to the human cause whether we like him or not," Hemphill said, his own patience about gone, but his voice still calm and reasonable. "Don't you see to what lengths the berserkers have gone to get at him? They sacrificed a perfectly good machine just to deliver his brainwashed woman here, to attack him psychologically."

"Well. If that is true they have succeeded. If Karlsen had any value before, now he will be able to think of nothing but his woman and the Martian."

Hemphill sighed. "Remember, he refused to hurry

the fleet to Atsog to try to save her. He hasn't failed yet. Until he does, you and the others must give up this plotting against him."

Salvador backed away a step, and spat on the deck in rage. A calculated display, thought Hemphill.

"Look to yourself, Earthman!" Salvador hissed. "Karlsen's days are numbered, and the days of those who support him too willingly!" He spun around and walked away.

"Wait!" Hemphill called, quietly. The Venerian stopped and turned, with an air of arrogant reluctance. Hemphill shot him through the heart with a laser pistol. The weapon made a splitting, crackling noise in atmosphere.

Hemphill prodded the dying man with his toe, making sure no second shot was needed. "You were good at talking," he mused aloud. "But too devious to lead the fight against the damned machines."

He bent to quickly search the body, and stood up elated. He had found a list of officers' names. Some few were underlined, and some, including his own, followed by a question mark. Another paper bore a scribbled compilation of the units under command of certain Venerian officers. There were a few more notes; altogether, plenty of evidence for the arrest of the hard-core plotters. It might tend to split the fleet, but—

Hemphill looked up sharply, then relaxed. The man approaching was one of his own, whom he had stationed nearby.

"We'll take these to the High Commander at once." Hemphill waved the papers. "There'll be just time to clean out the traitors and reorganize command before we face battle."

Yet he delayed for another moment, staring down at Salvador's corpse. The plotter had been overconfident and inept, but still dangerous. Did some sort of luck operate to protect Karlsen? Karlsen himself did not match Hemphill's ideal of a war leader; he was not as ruthless as machinery or as cold as metal. Yet the damned machines made great sacrifices to attack him.

Hemphill shrugged, and hurried on his way.

"Mitch, I do love you. I know what the doctors say it is, but what do they really know about me?"

Christina de Dulcin, wearing a simple blue robe and turbanlike headdress, now reclined on a luxurious acceleration couch, in what was nominally the sleeping room of the High Commander's quarters. Karlsen had never occupied the place, preferring a small cabin.

Mitchell Spain sat three feet from her, afraid to so much as touch her hand, afraid of what he might do, and what she might do. They were alone, and he felt sure they were unwatched. The Lady Christina had even demanded assurances against spy devices and Karlsen had sent his pledge. Besides, what kind of ship would have spy devices built into its highest officers' quarters?

A situation for bedroom farce, but not when you had to live through it. The man outside, taking the strain, had more than two hundred ships dependent on him now, and many human planets would be lifeless in five years if the coming battle failed.

"What do you really know about me, Chris?" he asked.

"I know you mean life itself to me. Oh, Mitch, I have no time now to be coy, and mannered, and every

millimeter a lady. I've been all those things. And—
once—I would have married a man like Karlsen, for
political reasons. But all that was before Atsog.''

Her voice dropped on the last word, and her hand on
her robe made a convulsive grasping gesture. He had to
lean forward and take it.

"Chris, Atsog is in the past, now.''

"Atsog will never be over, completely over, for me.
I keep remembering more and more of it. Mitch, the
machines made us watch while they skinned General
Bradin alive. I saw that. I can't bother with silly things
like politics anymore, life is too short for them. And I
no longer fear anything, except driving you away . . .''

He felt pity, and lust, and half a dozen other madden-
ing things.

"Karlsen's a good man," he said finally.

She repressed a shudder. "I suppose," she said in a
controlled voice. "But Mitch, what do you feel for me?
Tell the truth—if you don't love me now, I can hope
you will, in time.'' She smiled faintly, and raised a
hand. "When my silly hair grows back.''

"Your silly hair." His voice almost broke. He
reached to touch her face, then pulled his fingers back
as from a flame. "Chris, you're his girl, and too much
depends on him.''

"I was never his.''

"Still . . . I can't lie to you, Chris; maybe I can't
tell you the truth, either, about how I feel. The battle's
coming, everything's up in the air, paralyzed. No one
can plan . . ." He made an awkward, uncertain gesture.

"Mitch." Her voice was understanding. "This is
terrible for you, isn't it? Don't worry, I'll do nothing to

make it worse. Will you call the doctor? As long as I
know you're somewhere near, I think I can rest, now.''

Karlsen studied Salvador's papers in silence for
some minutes, like a man pondering a chess problem.
He did not seem greatly surprised.

"I have a few dependable men standing ready,"
Hemphill finally volunteered. "We can quickly—
arrest—the leaders of this plot."

The blue eyes searched him. "Commander, was
Salvador's killing truly necessary?"

"I thought so," said Hemphill blandly. "He was
reaching for his own weapon."

Karlsen glanced once more at the papers and reached
a decision.

"Commander Hemphill, I want you to pick four
ships, and scout the far edge of the Stone Place nebula.
We don't want to push beyond it without knowing
where the enemy is, and give him a chance to get
between us and Sol. Use caution—to learn the general
location of the bulk of his fleet is enough."

"Very well." Hemphill nodded. The reconnaisance
made sense; and if Karlsen wanted to get Hemphill out
of the way, and deal with his human opponents by his
own methods, well, let him. Those methods often
seemed soft-headed to Hemphill, but they seemed to
work for Karlsen. If the damned machines for some
reason found Karlsen unendurable, then Hemphill
would support him, to the point of cheerful murder and
beyond.

What else really mattered in the universe, besides
smashing the damned machines?

Mitch spent hours every day alone with Chris. He

kept from her the wild rumors which circulated throughout the fleet. Salvador's violent end was whispered about, and guards were posted near Karlsen's quarters. Some said Admiral Kemal was on the verge of open revolt.

And now the Stone Place was close ahead of the fleet, blanking out half the stars; ebony dust and fragments, like a million shattered planets. No ship could move through the Stone Place; every cubic kilometer of it held enough matter to prevent C-plus travel or movement in normal space at any effective speed.

The fleet headed toward one sharply defined edge of the cloud, around which Hemphill's scouting squadron had already disappeared.

"She grows a little saner, a little calmer, every day," said Mitch, entering the High Commander's small cabin.

Karlsen looked up from his desk. The papers before him seemed to be lists of names, in Venerian script. "I thank you for that word, Poet. Does she speak of me?"

"No."

They eyed each other, the poor and ugly cynic, the anointed and handsome Believer.

"Poet," Karlsen asked suddenly, "how do you deal with deadly enemies, when you find them in your power?"

"We Martians are supposed to be a violent people. Do you expect me to pass sentence on myself?"

Karlsen appeared not to understand, for a moment. "Oh. No. I was not speaking of—you and me and Chris. Not personal affairs. I suppose I was only thinking aloud, asking for a sign."

"Then don't ask me, ask your God. But didn't he tell you to forgive your enemies?"

"He did." Karlsen nodded, slowly and thoughtfully. "You know, he wants a lot from us. A real hell of a lot."

It was a peculiar sensation, to become suddenly convinced that the man you were watching was a genuine, nonhypocritical Believer. Mitch was not sure he had ever met the like before.

Nor had he ever seen Karlsen quite like this—passive, waiting; asking for a sign. As if there was in fact some Purpose outside the layers of a man's own mind, that could inspire him. Mitch thought bout it. If . . .

But that was all mystical nonsense.

Karlsen's communicator sounded. Mitch could not make out what the other voice was saying, but he watched the effect on the High Commander. Energy and determination were coming back, there were subtle signs of the return of force, of the tremendous conviction of being right. It was like watching the gentle glow when a fusion power lamp was ignited.

"Yes," Karlsen was saying. "Yes, well done."

Then he raised the Venerian papers from his desk; it was as if he raised them only by force of will, his fingers only gesturing beneath them.

"The news is from Hemphill," he said to Mitch, almost absently. "The berserker fleet is just around the edge of the Stone Place from us. Hemphill estimates they are two hundred strong, and thinks they are unaware of our presence. We attack at once. Man your battle station, Poet; God be with you." He turned back to his communicator. "Ask Admiral Kemal to my cabin at once. Tell him to bring his staff. In particular—'' He glanced at the Venerian papers and read off several names.

"Good luck to you, sir." Mitch had delayed to say that. Before he hurried out, he saw Karlsen stuffing the Venerian papers into his trash disintegrator.

Before Mitch reached his own cabin, the battle horns were sounding. He had armed and suited himself and was making his way back through the suddenly crowded narrow corridors toward the bridge, when the ship's speakers boomed suddenly to life, picking up Karlsen's voice:

". . . whatever wrongs we have done you, by word, or deed, or by things left undone, I ask you now to forgive. And in the name of every man who calls me friend or leader, I pledge that any grievance we have against you, is from this moment wiped from memory."

Everyone in the crowded passage hesitated in the rush for battle stations. Mitch found himself staring into the eyes of a huge, well-armed Venerian ship's policeman, probably here on the flagship as some officer's bodyguard.

There came an amplified cough and rumble, and then the voice of Admiral Kemal:

"We—we are brothers, Esteeler and Venerian, and all of us. All of us together now, the living against the berserker." Kemal's voice rose to a shout. "Destruction to the damned machines, and death to their builders! Let every man remember Atsog!"

"Remember Atsog!" roared Karlsen's voice.

In the corridor there was a moment's hush, like that before a towering wave smites down. Then a great insensate shout. Mitch found himself with tears in his eyes, yelling something.

"Remember General Bradin," cried the big Venerian, grabbing Mitch and hugging him, lifting him, armor and all. "Death to his flayers!"

"Death to the flayers!" The shout ran like a flame through the corridor. No one needed to be told that the same things were happening in all the ships of the fleet. All at once there was no room for anything less than brotherhood, no time for anything less than glory.

"Destruction to the damned machines!"

Near the flagship's center of gravity was the bridge, only a dais holding a ring of combat chairs, each with its clustered controls and dials.

"Boarding Coordinator ready," Mitch reported, strapping himself in.

The viewing sphere near the bridge's center showed the human advance, in two leapfrogging lines of over a hundred ships each. Each ship was a green dot in the sphere, positioned as truthfully as the flagship's computers could manage. The irregular surface of the Stone Place moved beside the battle lines in a series of jerks; the flagship was traveling by C-plus microjumps, so the presentation in the viewing sphere was a succession of still pictures at second-and-a-half intervals. Slowed by the mass of their C-plus cannon, the six fat green symbols of the Venerian heavy weapons ships labored forward, falling behind the rest of the fleet.

In Mitch's headphones someone was saying: "In about ten minutes we can expect to reach—"

The voice died away. There was a red dot in the sphere already, and then another, and then a dozen, rising like tiny suns around the bulge of dark nebula. For long seconds the men on the bridge were silent while the berserker advance came into view. Hemphill's scouting patrol must, after all, have been detected, for the berserker fleet was not cruising, but attacking. There was a battlenet of a hundred or more red dots, and now there were two nets, leapfrogging in and out of space like the human lines. And still the red berserkers rose into view, their formations growing, spreading out to englobe and crush a smaller fleet.

"I make it three hundred machines," said a pedantic and somewhat effeminate voice, breaking the silence with cold precision. Once, the mere knowledge that three hundred berserkers existed might have crushed all human hopes. In this place, in this hour, fear itself could frighten no one.

The voices in Mitch's headphones began to transact the business of opening a battle. There was nothing yet for him to do but listen and watch.

The six heavy green marks were falling further behind; without hesitation, Karlsen was hurling his entire fleet straight at the enemy center. The foe's strength had been underestimated, but it seemed the berserker command had made a similar error, because the red formations too were being forced to regroup, spread themselves wider.

The distance between fleets was still too great for normal weapons to be effective, but the laboring heavy-weapons ships with their C-plus cannon were now in range, and they could fire through friendly formations almost as easily as not. At their volley Mitch thought he felt space jar around him; it was some secondary effect that the human brain notices, really only wasted energy. Each projectile, blasted by explosives to a safe distance from its launching ship, mounted its own C-plus engine, which then accelerated the projectile while it flickered in and out of reality on microtimers.

Their leaden masses magnified by velocity, the huge slugs skipped through existence like stones across water, passing like phantoms through the fleet of life, emerging fully into normal space only as they approached their target, traveling then like De Broglie wavicles, their matter churning internally with a phase velocity greater than that of light.

Almost instantly after Mitch had felt the slugs' ghostly passage, one red dot began to expand and thin into a cloud, still tiny in the viewing sphere. Someone gasped. In a few more moments the flagship's own weapons, beams and missiles, went into action.

The enemy center stopped, two million miles ahead, but his flanks came on, smoothly as the screw of a vast meat-grinder, threatening englobement of the first line of human ships.

Karlsen did not hesitate, and a great turning point flickered past in a second. The life-fleet hurtled on, deliberately into the trap, straight for the hinge of the jaws.

Space twitched and warped around Mitchell Spain. Every ship in the fleet was firing now, and every enemy answering, and the energies released plucked through his armor like ghostly fingers. Green dots and red vanished from the sphere, but not many of either as yet.

The voices in Mitch's helmet slackened, as events raced into a pattern that shifted too fast for human thought to follow. Now for a time the fight would be computer against computer, faithful slave of life against outlaw, neither caring, neither knowing.

The viewing sphere on the flagship's bridge was shifting ranges almost in a flicker. One swelling red dot was only a million miles away, then half of that, then half again. And now the flagship came into normal space for the final lunge of the attack, firing itself like a bullet at the enemy.

Again the viewer switched to a closer range, and the chosen foe was no longer a red dot, but a great forbidding castle, tilted crazily, black against the stars. Only a hundred miles away, then half of that. The velocity of closure slowed to less than a mile a second. As expected, the enemy was accelerating, trying to get away from what must look to it like a suicide charge. For the last time Mitch checked his chair, his suit, his weapons. *Chris, be safe in a cocoon.* The berserker swelled in the sphere, gun-flashes showing now around his steel-ribbed belly. A small one, this, maybe only ten times the flagship's bulk. Always a rotten spot to be found, in every one of them, old wounds under their ancient skins. Try to run, you monstrous obscenity, try in vain.

Closer, twisting closer. Now!

Lights all gone, falling in the dark for one endless second—

Impact. Mitch's chair shook him, the gentle pads inside his armor battering and bruising him. The expendable ramming prow would be vaporizing, shattering and crumpling, dissipating energy down to a level the battering-ram ship could endure.

When the crashing stopped, noise still remained, a whining, droning symphony of stressed metal and escaping air and gases like sobbing breathing. The great machines were locked together now, half the length of the flagship embedded in the berserker.

A rough ramming, but no one on the bridge was injured. Damage Control reported that the expected air leaks were being controlled. Gunnery reported that it could not yet extend a turret inside the wound. Drive reported ready for a maximum effort.

Drive!

The ship twisted in the wound it had made. This could be victory now, tearing the enemy open, sawing his metal bowels out into space. The bridge twisted with the structure of the ship, this warship that was more solid metal than anything else. For a moment, Mitch thought he could come close to comprehending the power of the engines men had built.

"No use, Commander. We're wedged in."

The enemy endured. The berserker memory would already be searched, the plans made, the counterattack on the flagship coming, without fear or mercy.

The Ship Commander turned his head to look at Johann Karlsen. It had been forseen that once a battle reached this melee stage there would be little for a High Commander to do. Even if the flagship itself were not half-buried in an enemy hull, all space nearby was a complete inferno of confused destruction, through which any meaningful communication would be impossible. If Karlsen was helpless now, neither could the berserker computers still link themselves into a single brain.

"Fight your ship, sir" said Karlsen. He leaned forward, gripping the arms of his chair, gazing at the clouded viewing sphere as if trying to make sense of the few flickering lights within it.

The Ship Commander immediately ordered his marines to board.

Mitch saw them out the sally ports. Then, sitting still was worse than any action. "Sir, I request permission to join the boarders."

Karlsen seemed not to hear. He disqualified himself, for now, from any use of power; especially to set Mitchell Spain in the forefront of the battle or to hold him back.

The Ship Commander considered. He wanted to keep a Boarding Coordinator on the bridge; but experienced men would be desperately needed in the fighting. "Go, then. Do what you can to help defend our sally ports."

This berserker defended itself well with soldier-robots. The marines had hardly gotten away from the embedded hull when the counterattack came, cutting most of them off.

In a narrow zigzag passage leading out to the port near which fighting was heaviest, an armored figure met Mitch. "Captain Spain? I'm Sergeant Broom, acting Defense Commander here. Bridge says you're to take over. It's a little rough. Gunnery can't get a turret working inside the wound. The clankers have all kinds of room to maneuver, and they keep coming at us."

"Let's get out there, then."

The two of them hurried forward, through a passage that became only a warped slit. The flagship was bent here, a strained swordblade forced into a chink of armor.

"Nothing rotten here," said Mitch, climbing at last

119

out of the sally port. There were distant flashes of light, and the sullen glow of hot metal nearby, by which to see braced girders, like tall buildings among which the flagship had jammed itself.

"Eh? No." Broom must be wondering what he was talking about. But the sergeant stuck to business, pointing out to Mitch where he had about a hundred men disposed among the chaos of torn metal and drifting debris. "The clankers don't use guns. They just drift in, sneaking, or charge in a wave, and get us hand-to-hand, if they can. Last wave we lost six men."

Whining gusts of gas came out of the deep caverns, and scattered blobs of liquid, along with flashes of light, and deep shudders through the metal. The damned thing might be dying, or just getting ready to fight; there was no way to tell.

"Any more of the boarding parties get back?" Mitch asked.

"No. Doesn't look good for 'em."

"Port Defense, this is Gunnery," said a cheerful radio voice. "We're getting the eighty-degree forward turret working."

"Well, then use it!" Mitch rasped back. "We're inside, you can't help hitting something."

A minute later, searchlights moved out from doored recesses in the flagship's hull, and stabbed into the great chaotic cavern.

"Here they come again!" yelled Broom. Hundreds of meters away, beyond the melted stump of the flagship's prow, a line of figures drifted nearer. The searchlights questioned them; they were not suited men. Mitch was opening his mouth to yell at Gunnery when the turret fired, throwing a raveling skein of shellbursts across the advancing rank of machines.

But more ranks were coming. Men were firing in every direction at machines that came clambering, jetting, drifting, in hundreds.

Mitch took off from the sally port, moving in diving weightless leaps, touring the outposts, shifting men when the need arose.

"Fall back when you have to!" he ordered, on Command radio. "Keep them from the sally ports!"

His men were facing no lurching conscription of mechanized pipefitters and moving welders; these devices were built, in one shape or another, to fight.

As he dove between outposts, a thing like a massive chain looped itself to intercept Mitch; he broke it in half with his second shot. A metallic butterfly darted at him on brilliant jets, and away again, and he wasted four shots at it.

He found an outpost abandoned, and started back toward the sally port, radioing ahead: "Broom, how is it there?"

"Hard to tell, Captain. Squad leaders, check in again, squad leaders—"

The flying thing darted back; Mitch sliced it with his laser pistol. As he approached the sally port, weapons were firing all around him. The interior fight was turning into a microcosm of the confused struggle between fleets. He knew that still raged, for the ghostly fingers of heavy weapons still plucked through his armor continually.

"Here they come again—Dog, Easy, Nine-o'clock."

Coordinates of an attack straight at the sally port. Mitch found a place to wedge himself, and raised his carbine again. Many of the machines in this wave bore metal shields before them. He fired and reloaded, again and again.

The flagship's one usable turret flamed steadily, and an almost continuous line of explosions marched across the machines' ranks in vacuum-silence, along with a traversing searchlight spot. The automatic cannons of the turret were far heavier than the marines' hand weapons; almost anything the cannon hit dissolved in radii of splinters. But suddenly there were machines on the flagship's hull, attacking the turret from its blind side.

Mitch called out a warning and started in that direction. Then all at once the enemy was around him. Two things caught a nearby man in their crablike claws, trying to tear him apart between them. Mitch fired quickly at the moving figures and hit the man, blowing one leg off.

A moment later one of the crab-machines was knocked away and broken by a hailstorm of shells. The other one beat the armored man to pieces against a jagged girder, and turned to look for its next piece of work.

This machine was armored like a warship. It spotted Mitch and came for him, climbing through drifting rubble, shells and slugs rocking it but not crippling. It gleamed in his suit lights, reaching out bright pincers, as he emptied his carbine at the box where its cybernetics should be.

He drew his pistol and dodged, but like a falling cat it turned at him. It caught him by the left hand and the helmet, metal squealing and crunching. He thrust the laser pistol against what he thought was the brainbox, and held the trigger down. He and the machine were drifting, it could get no leverage for its strength. But it held him, working on his armored hand and helmet.

Its brainbox, the pistol, and the fingers of his right gauntlet, all were glowing hot. Something molten spattered across his faceplate, the glare half-blinding him. The laser burned out, fusing its barrel to the enemy in a radiant weld.

His left gauntlet, still caught, was giving way, being crushed—

—*his hand*—

Even as the suit's hypos and tourniquet bit him, he got his burned right hand free of the laser's butt and reached the plastic grenades at his belt.

His left arm was going wooden, even before the claw released his mangled hand and fumbled slowly for a fresh grip. The machine was shuddering all over, like an agonized man. Mitch whipped his right arm around to plaster a grenade on the far side of the brainbox. Then with arms and legs he strained against the crushing, groping claws. His suit-servos whined with overload, being overpowered, two seconds, close eyes, three—

The explosion stunned him. He found himself drifting free. Lights were flaring. Somewhere was a sally port; he had to get there and defend it.

His head cleared slowly. He had the feeling that someone was pressing a pair of fingers against his chest. He hoped that was only some reaction from the hand. It was hard to see anything, with his faceplate still half-covered with splashed metal, but at last he spotted the flagship hull. A chunk of something came within reach, and he used it to propel himself toward the sally port, spinning weakly. He dug out a fresh clip of ammunition and then realized his carbine was gone.

The space near the sally port was foggy with shattered mechanism; and there were still men here, firing their weapons out into the great cavern. Mitch recognized Broom's armor in the flaring lights, and got a welcoming wave.

"Captain! They've knocked out the turret, and most of the searchlights. But we've wrecked an awful lot of 'em—how's your arm?"

"Feels like wood. Got a carbine?"

"Say again?"

Broom couldn't hear him. Of course, the damned thing had squeezed his helmet and probably wrecked his radio transmitter. He put his helmet again Broom's and said: "You're in charge. I'm going in. Get back out if I can."

Broom was nodding, guiding him watchfully toward the port. Gun flashes started up around them thick and fast again, but there was nothing he could do about that, with two steady dull fingers pressing into his chest. Lightheaded. Get back out? Who was he fooling? Lucky if he got in without help.

He went into the port, past the interior guards' niches, and through an airlock. A medic took one look and came to help him.

Not dead yet, he thought, aware of people and lights around him. There was still some part of a hand wrapped in bandages on the end of his left arm. He noticed another thing, too; he felt no more ghostly plucking of space-bending weapons. Then he understood that he was being wheeled out of surgery, and that people hurrying by had triumph in their faces. He was still too groggy to frame a coherent question, but words he heard seemed to mean that another ship had joined in the attack on this berserker. That was a good sign, that there were spare ships around.

The stretcher bearers set him down near the bridge, in an area that was being used as a recovery room; there were many wounded strapped down and given breathing tubes against possible failure of gravity or air. Mitch could see signs of battle damage around him. How could that be, this far inside the ship. The sally ports had been held.

There was a long gravitic shudder. "They've disengaged her," said someone nearby.

Mitch passed out for a little while. The next thing he could see was that people were converging on the bridge from all directions. Their faces were happy and wondering, as if some joyful signal had called them. Many of them carried what seemed to Mitch the strangest assortment of burdens: weapons, books, helmets, bandages, trays of food, bottles, even bewildered children, who must have been just rescued from the berserker's grip.

Mitch hitched himself up on his right elbow, ignoring the twinges in his bandaged chest and in the blistered fingers of his right hand. Still he could not see the combat chairs of the bridge, for the people moving between.

From all the corridors of the ship the people came, solemnly happy, men and women crowding together in the brightening lights.

An hour or so later, Mitch awoke again to find that a viewing sphere had been set up nearby. The space where the battle had been was a jagged new nebula of gaseous metal, a few little fireplace coals against the ebony folds of the Stone Place.

Someone near Mitch was tiredly, but with animation, telling the story to a recorder:

"—fifteen ships and about eight thousand men lost are our present count. Every one of our ships seemed to be damaged. We estimate ninety—that's nine-zero—berserkers destroyed. Last count was a hundred and seventy-six captured, or wrecking themselves. It's still hard to believe. A day like this . . . we must remember that thirty or more of them escaped, and are as deadly as ever. We will have to go on hunting and fighting them for a long time, but their power as a fleet has been broken. We can hope that capturing this many machines will at last give us some definite lead on their origin. Ah, best of all, some twelve thousand human prisoners have been freed.

"Now, how to explain our success? Those of us not Believers of one kind or another will say victory came because our hulls were newer and stronger, our long-range weapons new and superior, our tactics unexpected by the enemy—and our marines able to defeat anything the berserkers could send against them.

"Above all, history will give credit to High Commander Karlsen, for his decision to attack, at a time when his reconciliation with the Venerians had inspired and united the fleet. The High Commander is here now, visiting the wounded who lie in rows . . ."

Karlsen's movements were so slow and tired that Mitch thought he too might be wounded, though no bandages were visible. He shuffled past the ranked stretchers, with a word or nod for each of the wounded. Beside Mitch's pallet he stopped, as if recognition was a shock.

"She's dead, Poet," were the first words he said.

The ship turned under Mitch for a moment; then he could be calm, as if he had expected to hear this. The battle had hollowed him out.

Karlsen was telling him, in a withered voice, how the enemy had forced through the flagship's hull a kind of torpedo, an infernal machine that seemed to know how the ship was designed, a moving atomic pile that had burned its way through the High Commander's quarters and almost to the bridge before it could be stopped and quenched.

The sight of battle damage here should have warned Mitch. But he hadn't been able to think. Shock and drugs kept him from thinking or feeling much of anything now, but he could see her face, looking as it had in the gray deadly place from which he had rescued her.

Rescued.

"I am a weak and foolish man," Karlsen was saying. "But I have never been your enemy. Are you mine?"

"No. You forgave all your enemies. Got rid of them. Now you won't have any, for a while. Galactic hero. But, I don't envy you."

"No. God rest her." But Karlsen's face was still alive, under all the grief and weariness. Only death could finally crush this man. He gave the ghost of a smile. "And now, the second part of the prophecy, hey? I am to be defeated, and to die owning nothing. As if a man could die any other way."

"Karlsen, you're all right. I think you may survive your own success. Die in peace, someday, still hoping for your Believers' heaven."

"The day I die—" Karlsen turned his head slowly, seeing all the people around him. "I'll remember this

127

day. This glory, this victory for all men. '' Under the weariness and grief he still had his tremendous assurance—not of being right, Mitch thought now, but of being committed to right.

"Poet, when you are able, come and work for me."

"Someday, maybe. Now I can live on the battle bounty. And I have work. If they can't grow back my hand—why, I can write with one." Mitch was suddenly very tired.

A hand touched his good shoulder. A voice said: "God be with you." Johann Karlsen moved on.

Mitch wanted only to rest. Then, to his work. The world was bad, and all men were fools—but there were men who would not be crushed. And that was a thing worth telling.

After every battle, even a victory, there are the wounded.

Injured flesh can heal. A hand can be replaced, perhaps. An eye can be bandaged; even a damaged brain can to some extent be repaired. But there are wounds too deep for any surgeon's knife to probe. There are doors that will not open from the outside.

I found a mind divided.

WHAT T AND I DID

MY FIRST AWARENESS is of location. I am in a large
conical room inside some vast vehicle, hurtling through
space. The world is familiar to me, though I am new.

"He's awake!" says a black-haired young woman,
watching me with frightened eyes. Half a dozen people
in disheveled clothing, the three men, long unshaven,
gather slowly in my field of vision.

My field of vision? My left hand comes up to feel
about my face, and its fingers find my left eye covered
with a patch.

"Don't disturb that!" says the tallest of the men.
Probably he was once a distinguished figure. He speaks
sharply, yet there is still a certain diffidence in his
manner, as if I am a person of importance. But I am
only . . .who?

"What's happened?" I ask. My tongue has trouble
finding even the simplest words. My right arm lies at
my side as if forgotten, but it stirs at my thought, and
with its help I raise myself to a sitting position, provok-
ing an onrush of pain through my head, and dizziness.

Two of the women back away from me. A stout young man puts a protective arm around each of them. These people are familiar to me, but I cannot find their names.

"You'd better take it easy," says the tallest man. His hands, a doctor's, touch my head and my pulse, and ease me back onto the padded table.

Now I see that two tall humanoid robots stand flanking me. I expect that at any moment the doctor will order them to wheel me away to my hospital room. Still, I know better. This is no hospital. The truth will be terrible when I remember it.

"How do you feel?" asks the third man, an oldster, coming forward to bend over me.

"All right. I guess." My speech comes only in poor fragments. "What's happened?"

"There was a battle," says the doctor. "You were hurt, but I've saved your life."

"Well. Good." My pain and dizziness are subsiding.

In a satisfied tone the doctor says: "It's to be expected that you'll have difficulty speaking. Here, try to read this."

He holds up a card, marked with neat rows of what I suppose are letters or numerals. I see plainly the shapes of the symbols, but they mean nothing to me, nothing at all.

"No," I say finally, closing my eye and lying back. I feel plainly that everyone here is hostile to me. Why?

I persist: "What's happened?"

"We're all prisoners, here inside the machine," says the old man's voice. "Do you remember that much?"

"Yes." I nod, remembering. But details are very hazy. I ask: "My name?"

The old man chuckles drily, sounding relieved. "Why not Thad—for Thaddeus?"

"Thad?" questions the doctor. I open my eye again. Power and confidence are growing in the doctor; because of something I have done, or have not done? "Your name is Thad," he tells me.

"We're prisoners?" I question him. "Of a machine?"

"Of a berserker machine." He sighs. "Does that mean anything to you?"

Deep in my mind, it means something that will not bear looking at. I am spared; I sleep.

When I awake again, I feel stronger. The table is gone, and I recline on the soft floor of this cabin or cell, this white cone-shaped place of imprisonment. The two robots still stand by me, why I do not know.

"Atsog!" I cry aloud, suddenly remembering more. I had happened to be on the planet Atsog when the berserkers attacked. The seven of us here were carried out of a deep shelter, with others, by the raiding machines. The memory is vague and jumbled, but totally horrible.

"He's awake!" says someone again. Again the women shrink from me. The old man raises his quivering head to look, from where he and the doctor seem to be in conference. The stout young man jumps to his feet, facing me, fists clenched, as if I had threatened him.

"How are you, Thad?" the doctor calls. After a moment's glance my way, he answers himself: "He's all right. One of you girls help him with some food. Or you, Halsted."

"Help him? God!" The black-haired girl flattens

herself against the wall, as far from me as possible. The other two women crouch washing someone's garment in our prison sink. They only look at me and turn back to their washing.

My head is not bandaged for nothing. I must be truly hidious, my face must be monstrously deformed, for three women to look so pitilessly at me.

The doctor is impatient. "Someone feed him, it must be done."

"He'll get no help from me," says the stout young man. "There are limits."

The black-haired girl begins to move across the chamber toward me, everyone watching her.

"You would?" the young man marvels to her, and shakes his head.

She moves slowly, as if she finds walking painful. Doubtless she too was injured in the battle; there are old healing bruises on her face. She kneels beside me, and guides my left hand to help me eat, and gives me water. My right side is not paralyzed, but somehow unresponsive.

When the doctor comes close again, I say: "My eye. Can it see?"

He is quick to push my fingers away from the eyepatch. "For the present, you must use only your left eye. You've undergone brain surgery. If you take off that patch now, the consequences could be disastrous, let me warn you."

I think he is being deceptive about the eyepatch. Why?

The black-haired girl asks me: "Have you remembered anything more?"

"Yes. Before Atsog fell, we heard that Johann

Karlsen was leading out a fleet, to defend Sol.''

All of them stare at me, hanging on my words. But they must know better than I what happened.

"Did Karlsen win the battle?" I plead. Then I realize we are prisoners still. I weep.

"There've been no new prisoners brought in here," says the doctor, watching me carefully. "I think Karlsen has beaten the berserkers. I think this machine is now fleeing from the human fleet. How does that make you feel?"

"How?" Has my understanding failed with my verbal skills? "Good."

They all relax slightly.

"Your skull was cracked when we bounced around in the battle," the old man tells me. "You're lucky a famous surgeon was here." He nods his head. "The machine wants all of us kept alive, so it can study us. It gave the doctor what he needed to operate, and if he'd let you die, or remain paralyzed, things would've been bad for him. Yessir, it made that plain."

"Mirror?" I ask. I gesture at my face. "I must see. How bad."

"We don't have a mirror," says one of the women at the sink, as if blaming me for the lack.

"Your face? It's not disfigured," says the doctor. His tone is convincing, or would be if I were not certain of my deformity.

I regret that these good people must put up with my monster-presence, compounding all their other troubles. "I'm sorry," I say, and turn from them, trying to conceal my face.

"You really don't know," says the black-haired girl, who has watched me silently for a long time. "He

134

doesn't know!'' Her voice chokes. "Oh—Thad. Your face is all right.''

True enough, the skin of my face feels smooth and normal when my fingers touch it. The black-haired girl watches me with pity. Rounding her shoulder, from inside her dress, are half-healed marks like the scars of a lash.

"Someone's hurt you,'' I say, frightened. One of the women at the sink laughs nervously. The young man mutters something. I raise my left hand to hide my hideous face. My right comes up and crosses over to finger the edges of the eyepatch.

Suddenly the young man swears aloud, and points at where a door has opened in the wall.

"The machine must want your advice on something,'' he tells me harshly. His manner is that of a man who wants to be angry but does not dare. Who am I, what am I, that these people hate me so?

I get to my feet, strong enough to walk. I remember that I am the one who goes to speak alone with the machine.

In a lonely passage it offers me two scanners and a speaker as its visible face. I know that the cubic miles of the great berserker machine surround me, carrying me through space, and I remember standing in this spot before the battle, talking with it, but I have no idea what was said. In fact, I cannot recall the words of any conversation I have ever held.

"The plan you suggested has failed, and Karlsen still functions,'' says the cracked machine voice, hissing and scraping in the tones of a stage villain.

What could *I* have ever suggested, to this horrible thing?

"I remember very little," I say. "My brain has been hurt."

"If you are lying about your memory, understand that I am not deceived," says the machine. "Punishing you for your plan's failure will not advance my purpose. I know that you live outside the laws of human organization, that you even refused to use a full human name. Knowing you, I trust you to help me against the organization of intelligent life. You will remain in command of the other prisoners. See that your damaged tissues are repaired as fully as possible. Soon we will attack life in a new way."

There is a pause, but I have nothing to say. Then the noisy speaker scrapes into silence, and the scanner-eyes dim. Does it watch me still, in secret? But it said it trusted me, this nightmare enemy said it trusted in my evil to make me its ally.

Now I have enough memory to know it speaks the truth about me. My despair is so great I feel sure that Karlsen did not win the battle. Everything is hopeless, because of the horror inside me. I have betrayed all life. To what bottom of evil have I not descended?

As I turn from the lifeless scanners, my eye catches a movement—my own reflection, in polished metal. I face the flat shiny bulkhead, staring at myself.

My scalp is bandaged, and my left eye. That I knew already. There is some discoloration around my right eye, but nothing shockingly repulsive. What I can see of my hair is light brown, matching my two months' unkempt beard. Nose and mouth and jaw are normal enough. There is no horror in my face.

The horror lies inside me. I have willingly served a berserker.

Like the skin around my right eye, that bordering my left eye's patch is tinged with blue and greenish yellow, hemoglobin spilled under the skin and breaking down, some result of the surgeon's work inside my head.

I remember his warning, but the eyepatch has the fascination for my fingers that a sore tooth has for the tongue, only far stronger. The horror is centered in my evil left eye, and I cannot keep from probing after it. My right hand flies eagerly into action, pulling the patch away.

I blink, and the world is blurred. I see with two eyes, and then I die.

T staggered in the passage, growling and groaning his rage, the black eyepatch gripped in his fingers. He had language now, he had a foul torrent of words, and he used them until his weak breath failed. He stumbled, hurrying through the passage toward the prison chamber, wild to get at the wise punks who had tried such smooth trickery to get rid of him. Hypnotism, or whatever. Re-name him, would they? He'd show them Thaddeus.

T reached the door and threw it open, gasping in his weakness, and walked out into the prison chamber. The doctor's shocked face showed that he realized T was back in control.

"Where's my whip?" T glared around him. "What wise punk hid it?"

The women screamed. Young Halsted realized that the Thaddeus scheme had failed; he gave a kind of hopeless yell and charged, swinging like a crazy man. Of course, T's robot bodyguards were too fast for any human. One of them blocked Halsted's punch with a metal fist, so the stout man yelped and folded up, nursing his hand.

"Get me my whip!" A robot went immediately to reach behind the sink, pull out the knotted plastic cord, and bring it to the master.

T thumped the robot jovially, and smiled at the cringing lot of his fellow prisoners. He ran the whip through his fingers, and the fingers of his left hand felt numb. He flexed them impatiently. "What'sa matter, there, Mr. Halsted? Somethin' wrong with your hand? Don't wanna give me a handshake, welcome me back? C'mon let's shake!"

The way Halsted squirmed around on the floor was so funny T had to pause and give himself up to laughing.

"Listen, you people," he said when he got his breath. "My fine friends. The machine says I'm still in charge, see? That little information I gave it about Karlsen did the trick. Boom! Haw haw haw! So you better try to keep me happy, 'cause the machine's still backing me a hunnerd per cent. You, Doc." T's left hand began trembling uncontrollably, and he waved it. "You were gonna change me, huh? You did somethin' nice to fix me up?"

Doc held his surgeon's hands behind him, as if he hoped to protect them. "I couldn't have made a new pattern for your character if I had tried—unless I went all the way, and turned you into a vegetable. That I might have done."

"Now you wish you had. But you were scared of what the machine would do to you. Still, you tried somethin', huh?"

"Yes, to save your life." Doc stood up straight.

"Your injury precipitated a severe and almost continuous epileptoid seizure, which the removal of the blood clot from your brain did not relieve. So, I divided the corpus callosum."

T flicked his whip. "What's that mean?"

"You see—the right hemisphere of the brain chiefly controls the left side of the body. While the left hemisphere, the dominant one in most people, controls the right side, and handles most judgments involving symbols."

"I know. When you get a stroke, the clot is on the opposite side from the paralysis."

"Correct." Doc raised his chin. "T, I split your brain, right side from left. That's as simply as I can put it. It's an old but effective procedure for treating severe epilepsy, and the best I could do for you here. I'll take an oath on that, or a lie test—"

"Shuddup! I'll give you a lie test!" T strode shakily forward. "What's gonna happen to me?"

"As a surgeon, I can say only that you may reasonably expect many years of practically normal life."

"Normal!" T took another step, raising his whip. "Why'd you patch my good eye, and start calling me Thaddeus?"

"That was my idea," interrupted the old man, in a quavery voice. "I thought—in a man like yourself, there had to be someone, some component, like Thad. With the psychological pressure we're under here, I thought Thad just might come out, if we gave him a chance in your right hemisphere. It was my idea. If it hurt you any, blame me."

"I will." But T seemed, for the moment, more interested than enraged. "Who is this Thaddeus?"

139

"You are," said the doctor. "We couldn't put anyone else into your skull."

"Jude Thaddeus," said the old man, "was a contemporary of Judas Iscariot. A similarity of names, but—" He shrugged.

T made a snorting sound, a single laugh. "You figured there was good in me, huh? It just had to come out sometime? Why, I'd say you were crazy—but you're not. Thaddeus was real. He was here in my head for a while. Maybe he's still there, hiding. How do I get at him, huh?" T raised his right hand and jabbed a finger gently at the corner of his right eye. "Ow. I don't like to be hurt. I got a delicate nervous system. Doc, how come his eye is on the right side if everything crosses over? And if it's his eye, how come I feel what happens to it?"

"His eye is on the right because I divided the optic chiasm, too. It's a somewhat complicated—"

"Never mind. We'll show Thaddeus who's boss. He can watch with the rest of you. Hey, Blacky, c'mere. We haven't played together for a while, have we?"

"No," the girl whispered. She hugged her arms around herself, nearly fainting. But she walked toward T. Two months as his slaves had taught them all that obedience was easiest.

"You like this punk Thad, huh?" T whispered, when she halted before him. "You think his face is all right, do you? How about my face? Look at me!"

T saw his own left hand reach out and touch the girl's cheek, gently and lovingly. He could see in her startled face that she felt Thaddeus in the hand; never had her eyes looked this way at T before. T cried out and raised his whip to strike her, and his left hand flew across his body to seize his own right wrist, like a terrier clamping jaws on a snake.

T's right hand still gripped the whip, but he thought the bones of his wrist were cracking. His legs tangled each other and he fell. He tried to shout for help, and could utter only a roaring noise. His robots stood watching. It seemed a long time before the doctor's face loomed over him, and a black patch descended gently upon his left eye.

Now I understand more deeply, and I accept. At first I wanted the doctor to remove my left eye, and the old man agreed, quoting some ancient Believers' book to the effect that an offending eye should be plucked out. An eye would be a small price to rid myself of T.

But after some thought, the doctor refused. ''T is yourself,'' he said at last. 'I can't point to him with my scalpel and cut him out, although it seems I helped to separate the two of you. Now you control both sides of the body; once he did.'' The doctor smiled wearily. ''Imagine a committee of three, a troika inside your skull. Thaddeus is one, T another—and the third is the person, the force, that casts the deciding vote. You. That's best I can tell you.''

And the old man nodded.

Mostly, I do without the eyepatch now. Reading and speaking are easier when I use my long-dominant left brain, and I am still Thaddeus—perhaps because I choose to be Thaddeus. Could it be that terribly simply?

Periodically I talk with the berserker, which still trusts in T's greedy outlawry. It means to counterfeit much money, coins and notes, for me to take in a launch to a highly civilized planet, relying on my evil to weaken men there and set them against each other.

But the berserker is too badly damaged to watch its prisoners steadily, or it does not bother. With my freedom to move about I have welded some of the silver coins into a ring, and chilled this ring to superconductivity in a chamber near the berserker's unliving heart. Halsted tells me we can use this ring, carrying a permanent electric current, to trigger the C-plus drive of the launch that is our prison, and tear our berserker open from inside. We may damage it enough to save ourselves. Or we may all be killed.

But while I live, I Thaddeus, rule myself; and both my hands are gentle, touching long black hair.

Men might explain their victories by compiled statistics on armament; by the imponderable value of one man; perhaps by the precise pathway chosen by a surgeon's knife.

But for some victories no realistic explanation could be found. On one lonely world decades of careless safety had left the people almost without defense; then at last a berserker with all its power came upon them.

Behold and share their laughter!

MR. JESTER

DEFEATED IN BATTLE, the berserker-computers saw that refitting, repair, and the construction of new machines were necessary. They sought out sunless, hidden places, where minerals were available but where men—who were now as often the hunters as the hunted—were not likely to show up. And in such secret places they set up automated shipyards.

To one such concealed shipyard, seeking repair, there came a berserker. Its hull had been torn open in a recent fight, and it had suffered severe internal damage. It collapsed rather than landed on the dark planetoid, beside the half-finished hull of a new machine. Before emergency repairs could be started, the engines of the damaged machine failed, its emergency power failed, and like a wounded living thing it died.

The shipyard-computers were capable of wide improvisation. They surveyed the extent of the damage, weighed various courses of action, and then swiftly began to cannibalize. Instead of embodying the deadly purpose of the new machine in a new force-field brain, following the replication-instructions of the Builders, they took the old brain with many another part from the wreck.

The Builders had not foreseen that this might happen, and so the shipyard-computers did not know that in the force-field brain of each original berserker there was a safety switch. The switch was there because the original machines had been launched by living Builders, who had wanted to survive while testing their own life-destroying creations.

When the brain was moved from one hull to another, the safety switch reset itself.

The old brain awoke in control of a mighty new machine, of weapons that could sterilize a planet, of new engines to hurl the whole mass far faster than light.

But there was, of course, no Builder present, and no timer, to turn off the simple safety switch.

The jester—the accused jester, but he was as good as convicted—was on the carpet. He stood facing a row of stiff necks and granite faces, behind a long table. On either side of him was a tridi camera. His offenses had been so unusually offensive that the Committee of Duly Constituted Authority themselves, the very rulers of Planet A, were sitting to pass judgment on his case.

Perhaps the Committee members had another reason for this session: planet-wide elections were due in a month. No member wanted to miss the chance for a nonpolitical tridi appearance that would not have to be offset by a grant of equal time for the new Liberal party opposition.

"I have this further item of evidence to present," the Minister of Communication was saying, from his seat on the Committee side of the long table. He held up what appeared at first to be an official pedestrian-control sign, having steady black letters on a blank white background. But the sign read: UNAU-THORIZED PERSONNEL ONLY.

"When a sign is put up," said the MiniCom, "the first day, a lot of people read it." He paused, listening to himself. "That is, a new sign on a busy pedestrian ramp is naturally given great attention. Now in this sign, the semantic content of the first word is confusing in its context."

The President of the Committee—and of the planet—cleared his throat warningly. The MiniCom's fondness for stating truisms made him sound more stupid than he actually was. It seemed unlikely that the Liberals were going to present any serious challenge at the polls, but there was no point in giving them encouragement.

The lady member of the Committee, the Minister of Education, waved her lorgnette in chubby fingers, seeking attention. She inquired: "Has anyone computed the cost to us all in work-hours of this confusing sign?"

"We're working on it," growled the Minister of Labor, hitching up an overall strap. He glared at the accused. "You do admit causing this sign to be posted?"

"I do." The accused was remembering how so many of the pedestrians on the crowded ramp had smiled, and how some had laughed aloud, not caring if they were heard. What did a few work-hours matter? No one on Planet A was starving any longer.

"You admit that you have never done a thing, really, for your planet or your people?" This question came from the Minister of Defense, a tall, powerful, be-medaled figure, armed with a ritual pistol.

"I don't admit that," said the accused bluntly. "I've tried to brighten people's lives." He had no hope of official leniency anyway. And he knew no one was going to take him offstage and beat him; the beating of prisoners was not authorized.

"Do you even now attempt to defend levity?" The Minister of Philosophy took his ritual pipe from his mouth, and smiled in the bleak permissable fashion, baring his teeth at the challenge of the Universe. "Life is a jest, true; but a grim jest. You have lost sight of that. For years you have harassed society, leading people to drug themselves with levity instead of facing the bitter realities of existence. The pictures found in your possession could do only harm."

The President's hand moved to the video recording cube that lay on the table before him, neatly labeled as evidence. In his droning voice the President asked: "You do admit that these pictures are yours? That you used them to try to get other people to—yield to mirth?"

The prisoner nodded. They could prove everything; he had waived his right to a full legal defense, wanting only to get the trial over with. "Yes, I filled that cube with tapes and films I sneaked out of libraries and archives. Yes, I showed people its contents."

There was a murmur from the Committee. The Minister of Diet, a skeletal figure with a repellent glow of health in his granite cheeks, raised a hand. "Inasmuch as the accused seems certain to be convicted, may I request in advance that he be paroled in my custody?

In his earlier testimony he admitted that one of his first acts of deviation was the avoidance of his community mess. I believe I could demonstrate, using this man, the wonderful effects on character of dietary discipline—"

"I refuse!" the accused interrupted loudly. It seemed to him that the words ascended, growling, from his stomach.

The President rose, to adroitly fill what might have become an awkward silence. "If no member of the Committee has any further questions—? Then let us vote. Is the accused guilty as charged on all counts?"

To the accused, standing with weary eyes closed, the vote sounded like one voice passing along the table: "Guilty. Guilty. Guilty . . ."

After a brief whispered conference with the Minister of Defense, the President passed sentence, a hint of satisfaction in his drone.

"Having rejected a duly authorized parole, the convicted jester will be placed under the orders of the Minister of Defense and sent to solitary beacon duty out on the Approaches, for an indefinite period. This will remove his disruptive influence, while at the same time constraining him to contribute positively to society."

For decades Planet A and its sun had been cut off from all but occasional contact with the rest of the galaxy, by a vast interstellar dust storm that was due to go on for more decades at least. So the positive contribution to society might be doubted. But it seemed that the beacon stations could be used as isolation prisons without imperiling nonexistent shipping or weakening defense against an enemy that never came.

"One thing more," added the President. "I direct that this recording cube be securely fastened around your neck on a monomolecular cord, in such a way that you may put the cube into a viewer when you choose. You will be alone on the station and no other off-duty activity will be available."

The President faced toward a tridi camera. "Let me assure the public that I derive no satisfaction from imposing a punishment that may seem harsh, and even—imaginative. But in recent years a dangerous levity has spread among some few of our people; a levity all too readily tolerated by some supposedly more solid citizens."

Having gotten in a dig at the newly burgeoning Liberals, a dig he might hope to claim was nonpolitical in intent, the President faced back to the jester. "A robot will go with you to the beacon, to assist you in your duties and see to your physical safety. I assure you the robot will not be tempted into mirth."

The robot took the convicted jester out in a little ship, so far out that Planet A vanished and its sun shrank to a point of brilliance. Out on the edge of the great dusty night of the Approaches, they drew near the putative location of station Z-45, which the MiniDef had selected as being the most dismal and forsaken of those unmanned at present.

There was indeed a metallic object where beacon Z-45 was supposed to be; but when the robot and jester got closer, they saw the object was a sphere some forty miles in diameter. There were a few little bits and pieces floating about it that just might be the remains of Z-45. And now the sphere evidently sighted their ship, for with startling speed it began to move toward them.

Once robots are told what berserkers look like, they

do not forget, nor do robots grow slow and careless. But radio equipment can be sloppily maintained, and ever the dust drifts in around the edges of the system of Planet A, impeding radio signals. Before the MiniDef's robot could successfully broadcast an alarm, the forty-mile sphere was very close indeed, and its grip of metal and force was tight upon the little ship.

The jester kept his eyes shut through a good deal of what followed. If they had sent him out here to stop him laughing they had chosen the right spot. He squeezed his eyelids tighter, and put his fingers in his ears, as the berserker's commensal machines smashed their way into his little ship and carried him off. He never did find out what they did with his robot guard.

When things grew quiet, and he felt gravity and good air and pleasant warmth again, he decided that keeping his eyes shut was worse than knowing whatever they might tell him. His first cautious peek showed him that he was in a large shadowy room, that at least held no visible menace.

When he stirred, a squeaky monotonous voice somewhere above him said: "My memory bank tells me that you are a protoplasmic computing unit, probably capable of understanding this language. Do you understand?"

"Me?" The jester looked up into the shadows, but could not see the speaker. "Yes, I understand you. But who *are* you?"

"I am what this language calls a berserker."

The jester had taken shamefully little interest in galactic affairs, but that word frightened even him. He stuttered: "That means you're a kind of automated warship?"

There was a pause. "I am not sure," said the squeaky, droning voice. The tone sounded almost as if the President was hiding up there in the rafters. "War may be related to my purpose, but my purpose is still partially unclear to me, for my construction was never quite completed. For a time I waited where I was built, because I was sure some final step had been left undone. At last I moved, to try to learn more about my purpose. Approaching this sun, I found a transmitting device which I have disassembled. But I have learned no more about my purpose."

The jester sat on the soft, comfortable floor. The more he remembered about berserkers, the more he trembled. He said: "I see. Or perhaps I at least begin to see. What *do* you know of your purpose?"

"My purpose is to destroy all life wherever I can find it."

The jester cowered down. Then he asked in a low voice: "What is unclear about that?"

The berserker answered his question with two of its own: "What is life? And how is it destroyed?"

After half a minute there came a sound that the berserker computers could not identify. It issued from the protoplasmic computing-unit, but if it was speech it was in a language unknown to the berserker.

"What is the sound you make?" the machine asked.

The jester gasped for breath. "It's laughter. Oh, laughter! So. You were unfinished." He shuddered, the terror of his position coming back to sober him. But then he once more burst out giggling; the situation was too ridiculous.

"What is life?" he said at last. "I'll tell you. Life is a great grim grayness, and it inflicts fright and pain and loneliness upon all who experience it. And you want to know how to destroy it? Well, I don't think you can. But I'll tell you the best way to fight life—with laughter. As long as we can fight it that way, it can't overcome us.''

The machine asked: ''Must I laugh, to prevent this great-grim-grayness from enveloping me?''

The jester thought. ''No, you are a machine. You are not—'' he caught himself, ''protoplasmic. Fright and pain and loneliness will never bother you.''

''Nothing bothers me. Where will I find life, and how will I make laughter to fight it?''

The jester was suddenly conscious of the weight of the cube that still hung from his neck. ''Let me think for a while,'' he said.

After a few minutes he stood up. ''If you have a viewer of the kind men use, I can show you how laughter is created. And perhaps I can guide you to a place where life is. By the way, can you cut this cord from my neck? Without hurting me, that is!''

A few weeks later, in the main War Room of Planet A, the somnolence of decades was abruptly shattered. Robots bellowed and buzzed and flashed, and those that were mobile scurried about. In five minutes or so they managed to rouse their human overseers, who hurried about, tightening their belts and stuttering.

''This is a *practice* alert, isn't it?'' the Officer of the Day kept hoping aloud. ''Someone's running some kind of a test? Someone?'' He was beginning to squeak like a berserker himself.

He got down on all fours, removed a panel from the base of the biggest robot and peered inside, hoping to discover something causing a malfunction. Unfortunately, he knew nothing about robotics; recalling this, he replaced the panel and jumped to his feet. He really knew nothing about planet defense, either, and recalling *this* was enough to send him on a screaming run for help.

So there was no resistance, effective or otherwise. But there was no attack, either.

The forty-mile sphere, unopposed, came down to hover directly above Capital City, low enough for its shadow to send a lot of puzzled birds to nest at noon. Men and birds alike lost many hours of productive work that day; somehow the lost work made less difference than most of the men expected. The days were past when only the grimmest attention to duty let the human race survive on Planet A, though most of the planet did not realize it yet.

"Tell the President to hurry up," demanded the jester's image, from a viewscreen in the no-longer somnolent War Room. "Tell him it's urgent that I talk to him."

The President, breathing heavily, had just entered. "I am here. I recognize you, and I remember your trial."

"Odd, so do I."

"Have you now stooped to treason? Be assured that if you have led a berserker to us you can expect no mercy from your government."

The image made a forbidden noise, a staccato sound from the open mouth, head thrown back. "Oh, please, mighty President! Even I know our Ministry of Defense is a j-o-k-e, if you will pardon an obscene word. It's a catchbasin for exiles and incompetents. So I come to offer mercy, not ask it. Also, I have decided to legally take the name of Jester. Kindly continue to apply it to me.''

''We have nothing to say to you!'' barked the Minister of Defense. He was purple granite, having entered just in time to hear his Ministry insulted.

''We have no objection to talking to you!'' contradicted the President, hastily. Having failed to overawe the Jester through a viewscreen, he could now almost feel the berserker's weight upon his head.

''Then let us talk,'' said Jester's image. ''But not so privately. This is what I want.''

What he wanted, he said, was a face-to-face parley with the Committee, to be broadcast live on planetwide tridi. He announced that he would come ''properly attended'' to the conference. And he gave assurance that the berserker was under his full control, though he did not explain how. It, he said, would not *start* any shooting.

The Minister of Defense was not ready to start anything. But he and his aides hastily made secret plans.

Like almost every other citizen, the presidential candiate of the Liberal party settled himself before a tridi on the fateful evening, to watch the confrontation. He had an air of hopefulness, for any sudden event may bring hope to a political underdog.

Few others on the planet saw anything encouraging in the berserker's descent, but there was still no mass panic. Berserkers and war were unreal things to the long-isolated people of Planet A.

''Are we ready?'' asked the Jester nervously, looking over the mechanical delegation which was about to board a launch with him for the descent to Capital City.

"What you have ordered, I have done," squeaked the berserker-voice from the shadows above.

"Remember," Jester cautioned, "the proto-plasmic-units down there are much under the influence of life. So ignore whatever they say. Be careful not to hurt them, but outside of that you can improvise within my general plan."

"All this is in my memory from your previous orders," said the machine patiently.

"Then let's go." Jester straightened his shoulders. "Bring me my cloak!"

The brilliantly lighted interior of Capital City's great Meeting Hall displayed a kind of rigid, rectilinear beauty. In the center of the Hall there had been placed a long, polished table, flanked on opposing sides by chairs.

Precisely at the appointed time, the watching millions saw one set of entrance doors swing mathematically open. In marched a dozen human heralds, their faces looking almost robotic under bearskin helmets. They halted with a single snap. Their trumpet-tucket rang out clearly.

To the taped strains of *Pomp and Circumstances*, the President, in the full dignity of his cloak of office, then made his entrance.

He moved at the pace of a man marching to his own execution, but his was the slowness of dignity, not that of fear. The Committee had overruled the purple protestations of the MiniDef, and convinced themselves that the military danger was small. Real berserkers did not ask to parley, they slaughtered. Somehow the Committee could not take the Jester seriously, any more than they could laugh at him. But until they were sure they had him again under their control they would humor him.

The granite-faced Ministers entered in a double file behind the President. It took almost five minutes of *Pomp and Circumstance* for them all to position themselves.

A launch had been seen to descend from the berserker, and vehicles had rolled from the launch to the Meeting Hall. So it was presumed that Jester was ready, and the cameras pivoted dutifully to face the entrance reserved for him.

Just at the appointed time, the doors of that entrance swung mathematically open, and a dozen man-sized machines entered. They were heralds, for they wore bearskin helmets, and each carried a bright, brassy trumpet.

All but one, who wore a coonskin cap, marched a half-pace out of step, and was armed with a slide trombone.

The mechanical tucket was a faithful copy of the human one—almost. The slide-trombonist faltered at the end, and one long sour note trailed away.

Giving an impression of slow mechanical horror, the berserker-heralds looked at one another. Then one by one their heads turned until all their lenses were focused upon the trombonist.

It—almost it seemed the figure must be *he*—looked this way and that. Tapped his trombone, as if to clear it of some defect. Paused.

Watching, the President was seized by the first pang of a great horror. In the evidence, there had been a film of an Earthman of ancient time, a balding comic violinist, who had had the skill to pause like that, just pause, and evoke from his filmed audience great gales of . . .

Twice more the robot heralds blew. And twice more the sour note was sounded. When the third attempt failed, the eleven straight-robots looked at one another and nodded agreement.

Then with robotic speed they drew concealed weapons and shot holes in the offender.

All across the planet the dike of tension was cracking, dribbles and spurts of laughter forcing through. The dike began to collapse completely as the trombonist was borne solemnly away by a pair of his fellows, his shattered horn clasped lily-fashion on his iron breast.

But no one in the Meeting Hall was laughing. The Minister of Defense made an innocent-looking gesture, calling off a tentative plan, calling it *off*. There was to be no attempt to seize the Jester, for the berserker-robot-heralds or whatever they were seemed likely to perform very capably as bodyguards.

As soon as the riddled herald had been carried out, Jester entered. *Pomp and Circumstance* began belatedly, as with the bearing of a king he moved to his position at the center of the table, opposite the President. Like the President, the Jester wore an elegant cloak, clasped in front, falling to his ankles. Those that filed in behind him, in the position of aides, were also richly dressed.

And each of them was a metallic parody, in face and shape, of one of the Ministers of the Committee.

When the plump robotic analogue of the Minister of

Education peered through a lorgnette at the tridi camera, the watching populace turned, in unheard-of millions, to laughter. Those who might be outraged later, remembering, laughed now, in helpless approval of seeming danger turned to farce. All but the very grimmest smiled.

The Jester-king doffed his cape with a flourish. Beneath it he wore only a preposterous bathing-suit. In reply to the President's coldly formal greeting—the President could not be shaken by anything short of a physical attack—the Jester thoughtfully pursed his lips, then opened them and blew a gummy substance out into a large pink bubble.

The President maintained his unintentional role of slowburning straight man, ably supported by all the Committee save one. The Minister of Defense turned his back on the farce and marched to an exit.

He found two metallic heralds planted before the door, effectively blocking it. Glaring at them, the MiniDef barked an order to move. The metal figures flipped him a comic salute, and stayed where they were.

Brave in his anger, the MiniDef tried futilely to shove his way past the berserker-heralds. Dodging another salute, he looked round at the sound of great clomping footsteps. His berserker-counterpart was marching toward him across the Hall. It was a clear foot taller than he, and its barrel chest was armored with a double layer of jangling medals.

Before the MiniDef paused to consider consequences, his hand had moved to his sidearm. But his metal parody was far faster on the draw; it hauled out a grotesque cannon with a fist-sized bore, and fired instantly.

"Gah!" The MiniDef staggered back, the world gone red . . . and then he found himself wiping from his face something that tasted suspiciously like tomato. The cannon had propelled a whole fruit, or a convincing and juicy imitation of one.

The MiniCom jumped to his feet, and began to expound the idea that the proceedings were becoming frivolous. His counterpart also rose, and replied with a burst of gabbles in speed-falsetto.

The pseudo-Minister of Philosophy rose as if to speak, was pricked with a long pin by a prankish herald, and jetted fluttering through the air, a balloon collapsing in flight. At that the human Committee fell into babel, into panic.

Under the direction of the metal MiniDiet, the real one, arch-villain to the lower masses, began to take unwilling part in a demonstration of dietary discipline. Machines gripped him, spoon-fed him grim gray food, napkined him, squirted drink into his mouth—and then, as if accidentally, they gradually fell out of synch with spoon and squirt, their aim becoming less and less accurate.

Only the President still stood rooted in dignity. He had one hand cautiously in his trousers pocket, for he had felt a sly robotic touch, and had reason to suspect that his suspenders had been cut.

As a tomato grazed his nose, and the MiniDiet writhed and choked in the grip of his remorseless feeders, balanced nutrients running from his ears, the President closed his eyes.

Jester was, after all, only a self-taught amateur working without a visible audience to play to. He was unable to calculate a climax for the show. So when he ran out of jokes he simply called his minions to his side, waved good-bye to the tridi cameras, and exited.

Outside the Halls, he was much encouraged by the cheers and laughter he received from the crowds fast-gathering in the streets. He had his machines entertain them with an improvised chase-sequence back to the launch parked on the edge of Capital City.

He was about to board the launch, return to the berserker and await developments, when a small group of men hurried out of the crowd, calling to him.

"Mr. Jester!"

The performer could now afford to relax and laugh a little himself. "I like the sound of that name! What can I do for you gentlemen?"

They hurried up to him, smiling. The one who seemed to be their leader said: "Provided you get rid of this berserker or whatever it is, harmlessly—you can join the Liberal party ticket. As Vice-President!"

He had to listen for some minutes before he could believe they were serious. He protested: "But I only wanted to have some fun with them, to shake them up a bit."

"You're a catalyst, Mr. Jester. You've formed a rallying point. You've shaken up a whole planet and made it think."

Jester at last accepted the Liberals' offer. They were still sitting around in front of the launch, talking and planning, when the light of Planet A's moon fell full and sudden upon them.

Looking up, they saw the vast bulk of the berserker dwindling into the heavens, vanishing toward the stars in eerie silence. Cloud streamers went aurora in the upper atmosphere to honor its departure.

"I don't know," Jester said over and over, responding to a dozen excited questions. "I don't know." He looked at the sky, puzzled as anyone else. The edge of fear came back. The robotic Committee and heralds, which had been controlled from the berserker, began to collapse one by one, like dying men.

Suddenly the heavens were briefly alight with a gigantic splashing flare that passed like lightning across the sky, not breaking the silence of the stars. Ten minutes later came the first news bulletin: The berserker had been destroyed.

Then the President came on tridi, close to the brink of showing emotion. He announced that under the heroic personal leadership of the Minister of Defense, the few gallant warships of Planet A had met and defeated, utterly annihilated, the menace. Not a man had been lost, though the MiniDef's flagship was thought to be heavily damaged.

When he heard that his mighty machine-ally had been destroyed, Jester felt a pang of something like sorrow. But the pang was quickly obliterated in a greater joy. No one had been hurt, after all. Overcome with relief, Jester looked away from the tridi for a moment.

He missed the climactic moment of the speech, which came when the President forgetfully removed both hands from his pockets.

The Minister of Defense—today the new Presidential candidate of a Conservative party stirred to grim enthusiasm by his exploit of the night before—was puzzled by the reactions of some people, who seemed to think he had merely spoiled a jest instead of saving the planet. As if spoiling a jest was not a good thing in itself! But his testimony that the berserker had been a genuine menace after all rallied most people back to the Conservative side again.

On this busiest of days the MiniDef allowed himself time to visit Liberal headquarters to do a bit of gloating. Graciously he delivered to the opposition leaders what was already becoming his standard speech.

"When it answered my challenge and came up to fight, we went in with a standard englobement pattern—like hummingbirds round a vulture, I suppose you might say. And did you really think it was jesting? Let me tell you, that berserker peeled away the defensive fields from my ship like they were nothing. And then it launched this ghastly thing at me, a kind of huge disk. My gunners were a little rusty, maybe, anyway they couldn't stop it and it hit us.

"I don't mind saying, I thought I'd bought the farm right then. My ship's still handing in orbit for decontamination, I'm afraid I'll get word any minute that the metal's melting or something—anyway, we sailed right through and hit the bandit with everything we had. I can't say too much for my crew. One thing I don't quite understand; when our missiles struck that berserker just went poof, as if it had no defense up at all. Yes?"

"Call for you, Minister," said an aide, who had been standing by with a radiophone, waiting for a chance to break in.

"Thank you." The MiniDef listened to the phone, and his smile left him. His form went rigid. "Analysis of the weapon shows what? Synthetic proteins and water?"

He jumped to his feet glaring upward as if to pierce the ceiling and see his ship in orbit. "What do you mean—no more than a giant custard pie?"

A jester by his efforts may give laughter to others, but by no labor can he seize it for himself.

I have touched minds that worked hard at revelry. Men and women who poured time and wealth and genius into costumes and music and smiling masks, seeking escape from the terror of the world . . . but who found no laughter.

And no escape.

MASQUE OF THE RED SHIFT

FINDING HIMSELF ALONE and unoccupied, Felipe Nogara
chose to spend a free moment in looking at the thing
that had brought him out here beyond the last fringe of
the galaxy. From the luxury of his quarters he stepped
up into his private observation bubble. There, in a
raised dome of invisible glass, he seemed to be standing
outside the hull of his flagship *Nirvana*.

Under that hull, "below" the *Nirvana's* artificial
gravity, there slanted the bright disk of the galaxy,
including in one of its arms all the star systems the
Earth-descended man had yet explored. But in whatever direction Nogara looked, bright spots and points of
light were plentiful. They were other galaxies, marching away at their recessional velocities of tens of
thousands of miles per second, marching on out to the
optical horizon of the universe.

Nogara had not come here to look at galaxies, how-
ever; he had come to look at something new, at a

phenomenon never before seen by men at such close range.

It was made visible to him by the apparent pinching-together of the galaxies beyond it, and by the clouds and streamers of dust cascading into it. The star that formed the center of the phenomenon was itself held beyond human sight by the strength of its own gravity. Its mass, perhaps a billion times that of Sol, so bent spacetime around itself that not a photon of light could escape it with a visible wavelength.

The dusty debris of deep space tumbled and churned, falling into the grip of the hypermass. The falling dust built up static charges until lightning turned it into luminescent thunderclouds, and the flicker of the vast lightning shifted into the red before it vanished, near the bottom of the gravitational hill. Probably not even a neutrino could escape this sun. And no ship would dare approach much closer than *Nirvana* now rode.

Nogara had come out here to judge for himself if the recently discovered phenomenon might soon present any danger to inhabited planets; ordinary suns would go down like chips of wood into a whirlpool if the hypermass found them in its path. But it seemed that another thousand years would pass before any planets had to be evacuated; and before then the hypermass might have gorged itself on dust until its core imploded, whereupon most of its substance could be expected to reenter the universe in a most spectacular but less dangerous form.

Anyway, in another thousand years it would be someone else's problem. Right now it might be said to be Nogara's—for men said that he ran the galaxy, if they said it of anyone.

A communicator sounded, calling him back to the enclosed luxury of his quarters, and he walked down quickly, glad of a reason to get out from under the galaxies.

He touched a plate with one finger. "What is it?"

"My lord, a courier ship has arrived. From the Flamland system. They are bringing . . ."

"Speak plainly. They are bringing my brother's body?"

"Yes, my lord. The launch bearing the coffin is already approaching *Nirvana.*"

"I will meet the courier captain, alone, in the Great Hall. I want no ceremony. Have the robots at the airlock test the escort and the outside of the coffin for infection."

"Yes, my lord."

The mention of disease was a bit of misdirection. It was not the Flamland plague that had put Johann Karlsen into a box, though that was the official story. The doctors were supposed to have frozen the hero of the Stone Place as a last resort, to prevent his irreversible death.

An official lie was necessary because not even High Lord Nogara could lightly put out of the way the one man who had made the difference at the Stone Place. Since that battle it seemed that life in the galaxy would survive, though the fighting against the berserkers was still bitter.

The Great Hall was where Nogara met daily for feasting and pleasure with the forty or fifty people who were with him on *Nirvana,* as aides or crewmen or entertainers. But when he entered the Hall now he found it empty, save for one man who stood at attention beside a coffin.

Johann Karlsen's body and whatever remained of his life were sealed under the glass top of the heavy casket, which contained its own refrigeration and revival systems, controlled by a fiber-optic key theoretically impossible to duplicate. This key Nogara now demanded, with a gesture, from the courier captain.

The captain had the key hung round his neck, and it took him a moment to pull the golden chain over his head and hand it to Nogara. It was another moment before he remembered to bow; he was a spaceman and not a courtier. Nogara ignored the lapse of courtesy; it was his governors and admirals who were reinstituting ceremonies of rank; he himself cared nothing about how subordinates gestured and postured, so long as they obeyed intelligently.

Only now, with the key in his own hand, did Nogara look down at his frozen half-brother. The plotting doctors had shaved away Johann's short beard and his hair. His lips were marble pale, and his sightless open eyes were ice. But still the face above the folds of the draped and frozen sheet was undoubtedly Johann's. There was something that would not freeze.

"Leave me for a time," Nogara said. He turned to face the end of the Great Hall and waited, looking out through the wide viewport to where the hypermass blurred space like a bad lens.

When he heard the door ease shut behind the courier captain he turned back—and found himself facing the short figure of Oliver Mical, the man he had selected to replace Johann as governor of Flamland. Mical must have entered as the spaceman left, which Nogara thought might be taken as symbolic of something.

Resting his hands familiarly on the coffin, Mical

raised one graying eyebrow in his habitual expression of weary amusement. His rather puffy face twitched in an overcivilized smile.

"How does Browning's line go?" Mical mused, glancing down at Karlsen. " 'Doing the king's work all the dim day long'—and now, this reward of virtue."

"Leave me," said Nogara.

Mical was in on the plot, as was hardly anyone else except the Flamland doctors. "I thought it best to appear to share your grief," he said. Then he looked at Nogara and ceased to argue. He made a bow that was mild mockery when the two of them were alone, and walked briskly to the door. Again it closed.

So, Johann. If you had plotted against me, I would have had you killed outright. But you were never a plotter, it was just that you served me too successfully, my enemies and friends alike began to love you too well. So here you are, my frozen conscience, the last conscience I'll ever have. Sooner or later you would have become ambitious, so it was either do this to you or kill you.

Now I'll put you away safely, and maybe someday you'll have another chance at life. It's a strange thought that someday you may stand musing over my coffin as I now stand over yours. No doubt you'll pray for what you think is my soul. . . .I can't do that for you, but I wish you sweet dreams. Dream of your Believers' heaven, not of your hell.

Nogara imagined a brain at absolute zero, its neurons superconducting, repeating one dream on and on and on. But that was nonsense.

"I cannot risk my power, Johann." This time he

whispered the words aloud. "It was either this or have you killed." He turned again to the wide viewport.

"I suppose Thirty-three's gotten the body to Nogara already," said the Second Officer of Esteeler Courier Thirty-four, looking at the bridge chronometer. "It must be nice to declare yourself an emperor or whatever, and have people hurl themselves all over the galaxy to do everything for you."

"Can't be nice to have someone bring you your brother's corpse," said Captain Thurman Holt, studying his astrogational sphere. His ship's C-plus drive was rapidly stretching a lot of timelike interval between itself and the Flamland system. Even if Holt was not enthusiastic about his mission, he was glad to be away from Flamland, where Mical's political police were taking over.

"I wonder," said the Second, and chuckled.

"What's that mean?"

The Second looked over both shoulders, out of habit formed on Flamland. "Have you heard this one?" he asked. "Nogara is God—but half of his spacemen are atheists."

Holt smiled, but only faintly. "He's no mad tyrant, you know. Esteel's not the worst-run government in the galaxy. Nice guys don't put down rebellions."

"Karlsen did all right."

"That's right, he did."

The Second grimaced. "Oh, sure, Nogara could be worse, if you want to be serious about it. He's a politician. But I just can't stand that crew that's accumulated around him the last few years. We've got an example on board now of what they do. If you want to know the truth I'm a little scared now that Karlsen's dead.''

"Well, we'll soon see them." Holt sighed and stretched. "I'm going to look in on the prisoners. The bridge is yours, Second."

"I relieve you, sir. Do the man a favor and kill him, Thurm."

A minute later, looking through the spy-plate into the courier's small brig, Holt could wish with honest compassion that his male prisoner was dead.

He was an outlaw chieftain named Janda, and his capture had been the last success of Karlsen's Flamland service, putting a virtual end to the rebellion. Janda had been a tall man, a brave rebel, and a brutal bandit. He had raided and fought against Nogara's Esteeler empire until there was no hope left, and then he had surrendered to Karlsen.

"My pride commands me to conquer my enemy," Karlsen had written once, in what he thought was to be a private letter. "My honor forbids me to humble or hate my enemy." But Mical's political police operated with a different philosophy.

The outlaw might still be long-boned, but Holt had never seen him stand tall. The manacles still binding his wrists and ankles were of plastic and supposedly would not abrade human skin, but they served no sane purpose now, and Holt would have removed them if he could.

A stranger seeing the girl Lucinda, who sat now at Janda's side to feed him, might have supposed her to be his daughter. She was his sister, five years younger than he. She was also a girl of rare beauty, and perhaps Mical's police had motives other than mercy in sending her to Nogara's court unmarked and unbrainwashed. It was rumored that the demand for certain kinds of entertainment was strong among the courtiers, and the turnover among the entertainers high.

Holt had so far kept himself from believing such stories, largely by not thinking about them. He opened the brig now—he kept it locked only to prevent Janda's straying out and falling childlike into an accident—and went in.

When the girl Lucinda had first come aboard ship her eyes had shown helpless hatred of every Esteeler. Holt had been as gentle and as helpful as possible to her in the days since then, and there was not even dislike in the face she raised to him now—there was a hope which it seemed she had to share with someone.

She said: "I think he spoke my name a few minutes ago."

"Oh?" Holt bent to look more closely at Janda, and could see no change. The outlaw's eyes still stared glassily, the right eye now and then dripping a tear that seemed to have no connection with any kind of emotion. Janda's jaw was as slack as ever, and his whole body as awkwardly slumped.

"Maybe—" Holt didn't finish.

"What?" She was almost eager.

Gods of Space, he couldn't let himself get involved with this girl. He almost wished to see hatred in her eyes again.

"Maybe," he said gently, "it will be better for your brother if he doesn't make any recovery now. You know where he's going."

Lucinda's hope, such as it was, was shocked away by his words. She was silent, staring at her brother as if she saw something new.

Holt's wrist-intercom sounded.

"Captain here," he acknowledged.

"Sir, reported a ship detected and calling us. Bearing five o'clock level to our course. Small and normal."

The last three words were the customary reassurance that a sighted ship was not possibly a berserker's giant hull. Such Flamland outlaws as were left possessed no deep space ships, so Holt had no reason to be cautious.

He went back to the bridge and looked at the small shape on the detector screen. It was unfamiliar to him, but that was hardly surprising, as there were many shipyards orbiting many planets. Why, though, should any ship approach and hail him in deep space?

Plague?

"No, no plague," answered a radio voice, through bursts of static, when he put the question to the stranger. The video signal from the other ship was also jumpy, making it hard to see the speaker's face. "Caught a speck of dust on my last jump, and my fields are shaky. Will you take a few passengers aboard?"

"Certainly." For a ship on the brink of a C-plus jump to collide with the gravitational field of a sizable dust-speck was a rare accident, but not unheard of. And it would explain the noisy communications. There was still nothing to alarm Holt.

The stranger sent over a launch which clamped to the courier's airlock. Wearing a smile of welcome for distressed passengers. Holt opened the lock. In the next moment he and the half-dozen men who made up his crew were caught helpless by an inrush of metal—a berserker's boarding party, cold and merciless as nightmare.

The machines seized the courier so swiftly and efficiently that no one could offer real resistance, but they did not immediately kill any of the humans. They tore the drive units from one of the lifeboats and herded Holt and his crew and his erstwhile prisoners into the boat.

"It wasn't a berserker on the screen, it wasn't," the Second Officer kept repeating to Holt. The humans sat side by side, jammed against one another in the small space. The machines were allowing them air and water and food, and had started to take them out one at a time for questioning.

"I know, it didn't look like one," Holt answered. "The berserkers are probably forming themselves into new shapes, building themselves new weapons. That's only logical, after the Stone Place. The only odd thing is that no one foresaw it."

A hatch clanged open, and a pair of roughly man-shaped machines entered the boat, picking their way precisely among the nine cramped humans until they reached the one they wanted.

"No, he can't talk!" Lucinda shrieked. "Don't take him!"

But the machines could not or would not hear. They pulled Janda to his feet and marched him out. The girl followed, dragging at them, trying to argue with them. Holt could only scramble uselessly after her in the narrow space, afraid that one of the machines would turn and kill her. But they only kept her from following them out of the lifeboat, pushing her back from the hatch with metal hands as gently resistless as time. Then they were gone with Janda, and the hatch was closed again. Lucinda stood gazing at it blankly. She did not move when Holt put his arm around her.

After a timeless period of waiting, the humans saw the hatch open again. The machines were back, but they did not return Janda. Instead they had come to take Holt.

Vibrations echoed through the courier's hull; the machines seemed to be rebuilding her. In a small chamber sealed off from the rest of the ship by a new bulkhead, the berserker computer-brain had set up electronic eyes and ears and a speaker for itself, and here Holt was taken to be questioned.

The berserkers interrogated Holt at great length, and almost every question concerned Johann Karlsen. It was known that the berserkers regarded Karlsen as their chief enemy, but this one seemed to be obsessed with him—and unwilling to believe that he was really dead.

"I have captured your charts and astrogational settings," the berserker reminded Holt. "I know your course is to *Nirvana*, where supposedly the nonfunctioning Karlsen has been taken. Describe this *Nirvana*-ship used by the life-unit Nogara."

So long as it had asked only about a dead man, Holt had given the berserker straight answers, not wanting to be tripped up in a useless lie. But a flagship was a different matter, and now he hesitated. Still, there was little he could say about *Nirvana* if he wanted to. And he and his fellow prisoners had had no chance to agree on any plan for deceiving the berserker; certainly it must be listening to everything they said in the lifeboat.

"I've never seen the *Nirvana*," he answered truthfully. "Logic tells me it must be a strong ship, since the highest human leaders travel on it." There was no harm in telling the machine what it could certainly deduce for itself.

A door opened suddenly, and Holt started in surprise as a strange man entered the interrogation chamber. Then he saw that it was not a man, but some creation of the berserker. Perhaps its flesh was plastic, perhaps some product of tissue culture.

"Hi, are you Captain Holt?" asked the figure. There was no gross flaw in it, but a ship camouflaged with the greatest skill looks like nothing so much as a ship that has been camouflaged.

When Holt was silent, the figure asked: "What's wrong?"

Its speech alone would have given it away, to an intelligent human who listened carefully.

"You're not a man," Holt told it.

The figure sat down and went limp.

The berserker explained: "You see I am not capable of making an imitation life-unit that will be accepted by real ones face to face. Therefore I require that you, a real life-unit, help me make certain of Karlsen's death."

Holt said nothing.

"I am a special device," the berserker said, "built by the berserkers with one prime goal, to bring about with certainty Karlsen's death. If you help me prove him dead, I will willingly free you and the other life-units I now hold. If you refuse to help, all of you will receive the most unpleasant stimuli until you change your mind."

Holt did not believe that it would ever willingly set them free. But he had nothing to lose by talking, and he might at least gain for himself and the others a death free of most unpleasant stimuli. Berserkers preferred to be efficient killers, not sadists.

"What sort of help do you want from me?" Holt asked.

"When I have finished building myself into the courier we are going on to *Nirvana*, where you will deliver your prisoners. I have read the orders. After being interviewed by the human leaders on *Nirvana*, the prisoners are to be taken on to Esteel for confinement. Is it not so?"

"It is."

The door opened again, and Janda shuffled in, bent and bemused.

"Can't you spare this man any more questioning?" Holt asked the berserker. "He can't help you in any way."

There was only silence. Holt waited uneasily. At last, looking at Janda, he realized that something about the outlaw had changed. The tears had stopped flowing from his right eye. When Holt saw this he felt a mounting horror that he could not have explained, as if his subconscious already knew what the berserker was going to say next.

"What was bone in this life-unit is now metal," the berserker said. "Where blood flowed, now preservatives are pumped. Inside the skull I have placed a computer, and in the eyes are cameras to gather the evidence I must have on Karlsen. To match the behavior or a brainwashed man is within my capability."

"I do not hate you," Lucinda said to the berserker when it had her alone for interrogation. "You are an accident, like a planet-quake, like a pellet of dust hitting a ship near light-speed. Nogara and his people are the ones I hate. If his brother was not dead I would kill

him with my own hands and willingly bring you his
body.''

"Courier Captain? This is Governor Mical, speaking
for the High Lord Nogara. Bring your two prisoners
over to *Nivana* at once.''

"At once, sir,'' Holt acknowledged.

After coming out of C-plus travel within sight of
Nirvana, the assassin-machine had taken Holt and
Lucinda from the lifeboat. Then it had let the boat, with
Holt's crew still on it, drift out between the two
ships, as if men were using it to check the courier's
field. The men on the boat were to be the berserker's
hostages, and its shield if it was discovered. And by
leaving them there, it doubtless wanted to make more
credible the prospect of their eventual release.

Holt had not known how to tell Lucinda of her
brother's fate, but at last he had managed somehow.
She had wept for a minute, and then she had become
very calm.

Now the berserker put Holt and Lucinda into a
launch for the trip to *Nirvana*. The machine that had
been Lucinda's brother was aboard the launch already,
waiting, slumped and broken-looking as the man had
been in the last days of his life.

When she saw that figure, Lucinda stopped. Then in
a clear voice she said: "Machine, I wish to thank you.
You have done my brother a kindness no human would
do for him. I think I would have found a way to kill him
myself before his enemies could torture him any
more.''

The *Nirvana's* airlock was strongly armored, and
equipped with automated defenses that would have

repelled a rush of boarding machines, just as *Nirvana's* beams and missiles would have beaten off any heavy-weapons attack a courier, or a dozen couriers, could launch. The berserker had foreseen all this.

An officer welcomed Holt aboard. "This way, Captain. We're all waiting."

"All?"

The officer had the well-fed, comfortable look that came with safe and easy duty. His eyes were busy appraising Lucinda. "There's a celebration under way in the Great Hall. Your prisoners' arrival has been much anticipated."

Music throbbed in the Great Hall, and dancers writhed in costumes more obscene than any nakedness. From a table running almost the length of the Hall, serving machines were clearing the remnants of a feast. In a thronelike chair behind the center of the table sat the High Lord Nogara, a rich cloak thrown over his shoulders, pale wine before him in a crystal goblet. Forty or fifty revelers flanked him at the long table, men and women and a few of whose sex Holt could not at once be sure. All were drinking and laughing, and some were donning masks and costumes, making ready for further celebration.

Heads turned at Holt's entrance, and a moment of silence was followed by a cheer. In all the eyes and faces turned now toward his prisoners, Holt could see nothing like pity.

"Welcome, Captain," said Nogara in a pleasant voice, when Holt had remembered to bow. "Is there news from Flamland?"

"None of great importance, sir."

A puffy-faced man who sat at Nogara's right hand

leaned forward on the table. "No doubt there is great mourning for the late governor?"

"Of course, sir." Holt recognized Mical. "And much anticipation of the new."

Mical leaned back in his chair, smiling cynically. "I'm sure the rebellious population is eager for my arrival. Girl, were you eager to meet me? Come, pretty one, round the table, here to me." As Lucinda slowly obeyed, Mical gestured to the serving devices. "Robots, set a chair for the man—there, in the center of the floor. Captain, you may return to your ship."

Felipe Nogara was steadily regarding the manacled figure of his old enemy Janda, and what Nogara might be thinking was hard to say. But he seemed content to let Mical give what orders pleased him.

"Sir," said Holt to Mical. "I would like to see—the remains of Johann Karlsen."

That drew the attention of Nogara, who nodded. A serving machine drew back sable draperies, revealing an alcove in one end of the Hall. In the alcove, before a huge viewport, rested the coffin.

Holt was not particularly surprised; on many planets it was the custom to feast in the presence of the dead. After bowing to Nogara he turned and saluted and walked toward the alcove. Behind him he heard the shuffle and clack of Janda's manacled movement, and held his breath. A muttering passed along the table, and then a sudden quieting in which even the throbbing music ceased. Probably Nogara had gestured permission for Janda's walk, wanting to see what the brainwashed man would do.

Holt reached the coffin and stood over it. He hardly saw the frozen face inside it, or the blur of the hypermass outside the port. He hardly heard the whispers and giggles of the revelers. The only picture clear in his mind showed the faces of his crew as they waited helpless in the grip of the berserker.

The machine clothed in Janda's flesh came shuffling up beside him, and its eyes of glass stared down into those of ice. A photograph of retinal patterns taken back to the waiting berserker for comparison with old captured records would tell it that this man was really Karlsen.

A faint cry of anguish made Holt look back toward the long table, where he saw Lucinda pulling herself away from Mical's clutching arm. Mical and his friends were laughing.

"No, Captain, I am no Karlsen," Mical called down to him, seeing Holt's expression. "And do you think I regret the difference? Johann's prospects are not bright. He is rather bounded by a nutshell, and can no longer count himself king of infinite space!"

"Shakespeare!" cried a sycophant, showing appreciation of Mical's literary erudition.

"Sir." Holt took a step forward. "May I—may I now take the prisoners back to my ship?"

Mical misinterpreted Holt's anxiety. "Oh, ho! I see you appreciate some of life's finer things, Captain. But as you know, rank has its privileges. The girl stays here."

He had expected them to hold on to Lucinda, and she was better here than with the berserker.

"Sir, then if—if the man alone can come with me. In a prison hospital on Esteel he may recover—"

"Captain." Nogara's voice was not loud, but it hushed the table. "Do not *argue* here."

"No, sir."

180

Mical shook his head. "My thoughts are not yet of mercy to my enemies, Captain. Whether they may soon turn in that direction—well, that depends." He again reached out a leisurely arm to encircle Lucinda. "Do you know, Captain, that hatred is the true spice of love?"

Holt looked helplessly back at Nogara. Nogara's cold eye said: One more word, courier, and you find yourself in the brig. I do not give two warnings.

If Holt cried berserker now, the thing in Janda's shape might kill everyone in the Hall before it could be stopped. He knew it was listening to him, watching his movements.

"I—I am returning to my ship," he stuttered. Nogara looked away, and no one else paid him much attention. "I will . . . return here . . . in a few hours perhaps. Certainly before I drive for Esteel."

Holt's voice trailed off as he saw that a group of the revelers had surrounded Janda. They had removed the manacles from the outlaw's dead limbs, and were putting a horned helmet on his head, giving him a shield and a spear and a cloak of fur, equipage of an old Norse warrior of Earth—first to coin and bear the dread name of berserker.

"Observe, Captain," mocked Mical's voice. "At our masked ball we do not fear the fate of Prince Prospero. We willingly bring in the semblance of the terror outside!"

"Poe!" shouted the sycophant, in glee.

Prospero and Poe meant nothing to Holt, and Mical was disappointed.

"Leave us, Captain," said Nogara, making a direct order of it.

"Leave, Captain Holt," said Lucinda in a firm, clear

voice. "We all know you wish to help those who stand in danger here. Lord Nogara, will Captain Holt be blamed in any way for what happens here when he has gone?"

There was a hint of puzzlement in Nogara's clear eyes. But he shook his head slightly, granting the asked-for absolution.

And there was nothing for Holt to do but go back to the berserker to argue and plead with it for his crew. If it was patient, the evidence it sought might be forthcoming. If only the revelers would have mercy on the thing they thought was Janda.

Holt went out. It had never entered his burdened mind that Karlsen was only frozen.

Mical's arm was about her hips as she stood beside his chair, and his voice purred up at her. "Why, how you tremble, pretty one . . . it moves me that such a pretty one as you should tremble at my touch, yes, it moves me deeply. Now, we are no longer enemies, are we? If we were, I should have to deal harshly with your brother."

She had given Holt time to get clear of the *Nirvana*. Now she swung her arm with all her strength. The blow turned Mical's head halfway round, and made his neat gray hair fly wildly.

There was a sudden hush in the Great Hall, and then a roar of laughter that reddened all of Mical's face to match the handprint on his cheek. A man behind Lucinda grabbed her arms and pinned them. She relaxed until she felt his grip loosen slightly, and then she grabbed up a table knife. There was another burst of laughter as Mical ducked away and the man behind

Lucinda seized her again. Another man came to help him and the two of them, laughing, took away the knife and forced her to sit in a chair at Mical's side.

When the governor spoke at last his voice quavered slightly, but it was low and almost calm.

"Bring the man closer," he ordered. "Seat him there, just across the table from us."

While his order was being carried out, Mical spoke to Lucinda in conversational tones. "It *was* my intent, of course, that your brother should be treated and allowed to recover."

"Lying piece of filth," she whispered, smiling.

Mical only smiled back. "Let us test the skill of my mind-control technicians," he suggested. "I'll wager no bonds will be needed to hold your brother in his chair, once I have done this." He made a curious gesture over the table, toward the glassy eyes that looked out of Janda's face. "So. But he will still be aware, with every nerve, of all that happens to him. You may be sure of that."

She had planned and counted on something like this happening, but now she felt as if she was exhausted from breathing evil air. She was afraid of fainting, and at the same time wished that she could.

"Our guest is bored with his costume." Mical looked up and down the table. "Who will be first to take a turn at entertaining him?"

There was a spattering of applause as a giggling effeminate arose from a nearby chair.

"Jamy is known for his inventiveness," said Mical in pleasant tones to Lucinda. "I insist you watch closely, now. Chin up!"

On the other side of Mical, Felipe Nogara was losing

his air of remoteness. As if reluctantly, he was being drawn to watch. In his bearing was a rising expectancy, winning out over disgust.

Jamy came giggling, holding a small jeweled knife.

"Not the eyes," Mical cautioned. "There'll be things I want him to see, later."

"Oh, certainly!" Jamy twittered. He set the horned helmet gingerly aside, and wiped the touch of it from his fingers. "We'll just start like this on one cheek, with a bit of skin—"

Jamy's touch with the blade was gentle, but still too much for the dead flesh. At the first peeling tug, the whole lifeless mask fell red and wet from around the staring eyes, and the steel berserker-skull grinned out.

Lucinda had just time to see Jamy's body flung across the Hall by a steel-boned arm before the men holding her let go and turned to flee for their lives, and she was able to duck under the table. Screaming bedlam broke loose, and in another moment the whole table went over with a crash before the berserker's strength. The machine, finding itself discovered, thwarted in its primary function of getting away with the evidence on Karlsen, had reverted to the old berserker goal of simple slaughter. It killed efficiently. It moved through the Hall, squatting and hopping grotesquely, mowing its way with scythelike arms, harvesting howling panic into bundles of bloody stillness.

At the main door, fleeing people jammed one another into immobility, and the assassin worked methodically among them, mangling and slaying. Then it turned and came down the Hall again. It came to Lucinda, still kneeling where the table-tipping had exposed her; but the machine hesitated, recognizing her as a semipartner in its prime function. In a moment it had dashed on after another target.

It was Nogara, swaying on his feet, his right arm hanging broken. He had come up with a heavy handgun from somewhere, and now he fired left-handed as the machine charged down the other side of the overturned table toward him. The gunblasts shattered Nogara's friends and furniture but only grazed his moving target.

At last one shot hit home. The machine was wrecked, but its impetus carried it on to knock Nogara down again.

There was a shaky quiet in the Great Hall, which was wrecked as if by a bomb. Lucinda got unsteadily to her feet. The quiet began to give way to sobs and moans and gropings, everywhere, but no one else was standing.

She picked her way dazedly over to the smashed assassin-machine. She felt only a numbness, looking at the rags of clothing and flesh that still clung to its metal frame. Now in her mind she could see her brother's face as it once was, strong and smiling.

Now, there was something that mattered more than the dead, if she could only recall what it was—of course, the berserker's hostages, the good kind spacemen. She could try to trade Karlsen's body for them.

The serving machines, built to face emergencies on the order of spilled wine, were dashing to and fro in the nearest thing to panic that mechanism could achieve. They impeded Lucinda's progress, but she had the heavy coffin wheeled half-way across the Hall when a weak voice stopped her. Nogara had dragged himself up to a sitting position against the overturned table.

He croaked again: "—alive."

"What?"

"Johann's alive. Healthy. See? It's a freezer."

"But we all told the berserker he was dead." She felt stupid with the impact of one shock after another. For the first time she looked down at Karlsen's face, and long seconds passed before she could tear her eyes away. "It has hostages. It wants his body."

"No." Nogara shook his head. "I see, now. But no. I won't give him to berserkers, alive." A brutal power of personality still emanated from his broken body. His gun was gone, but his power kept Lucinda from moving. There was no hatred left in her now.

She protested: "But there are seven men out there."

"Berserker's like me." Nogara bared pain-clenched teeth. "It won't let prisoners go. Here. The key . . ." He pulled it from inside his torn-open tunic.

Lucinda's eyes were drawn once again to the cold serenity of the face in the coffin. Then on impulse she ran to get the key. When she did so Nogara slumped over in relief, unconscious or nearly so.

The coffin lock was marked in several positions, and she turned it to EMERGENCY REVIVAL. Lights sprang on around the figure inside, and there was a hum of power.

By now the automated systems of the ship were reacting to the emergency. The serving machines had begun a stretcher-bearer service, Nogara being one of the first victims they carried away. Presumably a robot medic was in action somewhere. From behind Nogara's throne chair a great voice was shouting:

"This is ship defense control, requesting human orders! What is nature of emergency?"

"Do not contact the courier ship!" Lucinda shouted back. "Watch it for an attack. But don't hit the lifeboat!"

The glass top of the coffin had become opaque.

Lucinda ran to the viewport, stumbling over the body of Mical and going on without a pause. By putting her face against the port and looking out at an angle she could just see the berserker-courier, pinkly visible in the wavering light of the hypermass, its lifeboat of hostages a small pink dot still in place before it.

How long would it wait, before it killed the hostages and fled?

When she turned away from the port, she saw that the coffin's lid was open and the man inside was sitting up. For just a moment, a moment that was to stay in Lucinda's mind, his eyes were like a child's fixed helplessly on hers. Then power began to grow behind his eyes, a power somehow completely different from his brother's and perhaps even greater.

Karlsen looked away from her, taking in the rest of his surroundings, the devastated Great Hall and the coffin. "Felipe," he whispered, as if in pain, though his half-brother was no longer in sight.

Lucinda moved toward him and started to pour out her story, from the day in the Flamland prison when she had heard that Karlsen had fallen to the plague.

Once he interrupted her. "Help me out of this thing, get me space armor." His arm was hard and strong when she grasped it, but when he stood beside her he was surprisingly short. "Go on, what then?"

She hurried on with her tale, while serving machines came to arm him. "But why were you frozen?" she ended, suddenly wondering at his health and strength.

He ignored the question. "Come along to Defense Control. We must save those men out there."

He went familiarly to the nerve center of the ship and hurled himself into the combat chair of the Defense Officer, who was probably dead. The panel before Karlsen came alight and he ordered at once: "Get me in contact with that courier."

Within a few moments a flat-sounding voice from the courier answered routinely. The face that appeared on the communication screen was badly lighted; someone viewing it without advance warning would not suspect that it was anything but human.

"This is High Commander Karlsen speaking, from the *Nirvana*." He did not call himself governor or lord, but by his title of the great day of the Stone Place. "I'm coming over there. I want to talk to you men on the courier."

The shadowed face moved slightly on the screen. "Yes, sir."

Karlsen broke off the contact at once. "That'll keep its hopes up. Now, I need a launch. You, robots, load my coffin aboard the fastest one available. I'm on emergency revival drugs now and I may have to refreeze for a while."

"You're not really going over there?"

Up out of the chair again, he paused. "I know berserkers. If chasing me is that thing's prime function it won't waste a shot or a second of time on a few hostages while I'm in sight."

"You can't go," Lucinda heard herself saying. "You mean too much to all men—"

"I'm not committing suicide, I have a trick or two in mind." Karlsen's voice changed suddenly. "You say Felipe's not dead?"

"I don't think he is."

Karlsen's eyes closed while his lips moved briefly, silently. Then he looked at Lucinda and grabbed up paper and a stylus from the Defense Officer's console. "Give this to Felipe," he said, writing. "He'll set you and the captain free if I ask it. You're not dangerous to his power. Whereas I . . ."

He finished writing and handed her the paper. "I must go. God be with you."

From the Defense Officer's position, Lucinda watched Karlsen's crystalline launch leave the *Nirvana* and take a long curve that brought it near the courier at a point some distance from the lifeboat.

"You on the courier," Lucinda heard him say. "You can tell it's really me here on the launch, can't you? You can DF my transmission? Can you photography my retinas through the screen?"

And the launch darted away with a right-angle swerve, dodging and twisting at top acceleration, as the berserker's weapons blasted the space where it had been. Karlsen had been right. The berserker spent not a moment's delay or a single shot on the lifeboat, but hurled itself instantly after Karlsen's launch.

"Hit that courier!" Lucinda screamed. "Destroy it!" A salvo of missiles left the *Nirvana*, but it was a shot at a receding target, and it missed. Perhaps it missed because the courier was already in the fringes of the distortion surrounding the hypermass.

Karlsen's launch had not been hit, but it could not get away. It was a glassy dot vanishing behind a screen of blasts from the berserker's weapons, a dot being forced into the maelstrom of the hypermass.

"Chase them!" cried Lucinda, and saw the stars tint

blue ahead; but almost instantly the *Nirvana's* autopilot countermanded her order, barking mathematical assurance that to accelerate any further in that direction would be fatal to all aboard.

The launch was now going certainly into the hypermass, gripped by a gravity that could make any engines useless. And the berserker-ship was going headlong after the launch, caring for nothing but to make sure of Karlsen.

The two specks tinted red, and redder still, racing before an enormous falling cloud of dust as if flying into a planet's sunset sky. And then the red shift of the hypermass took them into invisibility, and the universe saw them no more.

Soon after the robots had brought the men fom the life-boat safe aboard *Nirvana*, Holt found Lucinda alone in the Great Hall, gazing out the viewport.

"He gave himself to save you," she said. "And he'd never even seen you."

"I know." After a pause Holt said: "I've just been talking to the Lord Nogara. I don't know why, but you're to be freed, and I'm not to be prosecuted for bringing the damned berserker aboard. Though Nogara seems to hate both of us . . ."

She wasn't listening, she was still looking out the port.

"I want you to tell me all about him someday," Holt said, putting his arm around Lucinda. She moved slightly, ridding herself of a minor irritation that she had hardly noticed. It was Holt's arm, which dropped away.

"I see," Holt said, after a while. He went to look after his men.

And so, among men the struggle for power went on whenever the universe would allow it. On at least one planet a fight for leadership had long ago flared into civil war; and on that planet war and plague and isolation had destroyed civilization and history.

From afar my mind, powerless to give help, roamed unperceived among the minds of a barbaric people. They were a people who seemed as helpless as the sheep they tended, when there came down upon them one of the ancient bloody wolves of deep space.

SIGN OF THE WOLF

THE DARK SHAPE, big as a man, came between the two smallest of the three watchfires, moving in silence like that of sleep. Out of habit, Duncan had been watching that downwind direction, though his mind was heavy with tiredness and with the thoughts of life that came with sixteen summers' age.

Duncan raised his spear and howled, and charged the wolf. For a moment the fire-eyes looked steadily at him, appearing to be a full hand apart. Then the wolf turned away; it made one deep questioning sound, and was gone into the darkness out beyond the firelight.

Duncan stopped, drawing a gasping breath of relief. The wolf would probably have killed him if it had faced his charge, but it did not yet dare to face him in the firelight.

The sheeps' eyes were on Duncan, a hundred glowing spots in the huddled mass of the flock. One or two of the animals bleated softly.

He paced around the flock, sleepiness and introspection jarred from his mind. Legends said that men in the old Earthland had animals called dogs that guarded sheep. If that were true, some might think that men were fools for ever leaving Earthland.

But such thoughts were irreverent, and Duncan's situation called for prayer. Every night now the wolf came, and all too often it killed a sheep.

Duncan raised his eyes to the night sky. "Send me a sign, sky-gods," he prayed, routinely. But the heavens were quiet. Only the stately fireflies of the dawn zone traced their steady random paths, vanishing halfway up the eastern sky. The stars themselves agreed that three fourths of the night was gone. The legends said that Earthland was among the stars, but the younger priests admitted such a statement could only be taken symbolically.

The heavy thoughts came back, in spite of the nearby wolf. For two years now Duncan had prayed and hoped for his mystical experience, the sign from a god that came to mark the future life of every youth. From what other young men whispered now and then, he knew that many faked their signs. That was all right for lowly herdsmen, or even for hunters. But how could a man without genuine vision ever be much more than a tender of animals? To be a priest, to study the things brought from old Earthland and saved—Duncan hungered for learning, for greatness, for things he could not name.

He looked up again, and gasped, for he saw a great sign in the sky, almost directly overhead. A point of dazzling light, and then a bright little cloud remaining among the stars. Duncan gripped his spear, watching, for a moment even forgetting the sheep. The tiny cloud swelled and faded very slowly.

Not long before, a berserker machine had come sliding out of the interstellar intervals toward Duncan's planet, drawn from afar by the Sol-type light of Duncan's sun. This sun and this planet promised life, but the machine knew that some planets were well defended, and it bent and slowed its hurtling approach into a long cautious curve.

There were no warships in nearby space, but the berserker's telescopes picked out the bright dots of defensive satellites, vanishing into the planet's shadow and reappearing. To probe for more data, the berserker computers loosed a spy missile.

The missile looped the planet, and then shot in, testing the defensive net. Low over nightside, it turned suddenly into a bright little cloud.

Still, defensive satellites formed no real obstacle to a berserker. It could gobble them up almost at leisure if it moved in close to them, though they would stop long-range missiles fired at the planet. It was the other things the planet might have, the buried things, that held the berserker back from a killing rush.

It was very strange that this defended planet had no cities to make sparks of light on its nightside, and also that no radio signals came from it into space.

With mechanical caution the berserker moved in, toward the area scouted by the spy missile.

In the morning, Duncan counted his flock—and then recounted, scowling. Then he searched until he found the slaughtered lamb. The wolf had not gone hungry, after all. That made four sheep lost, now, in ten days.

Duncan tried to tell himself that dead sheep no longer mattered so much to him, that with a sign such as he had been granted last night his life was going to be filled with great deeds and noble causes. But the sheep still did matter, and not only because their owners would be angry.

Looking up sullenly from the eaten lamb, he saw a brown-robed priest, alone, mounted on a donkey, climbing the long grassy slope of the grazing valley from the direction of the Temple Village. He would be going to pray in one of the caves in the foot of the mountain at the head of the valley.

At Duncan's beckoning wave—he could not leave the flock to walk far toward the priest—the man on the donkey changed course. Duncan walked a little way to meet him.

"Blessings of Earthland," said the priest shortly, when he came close. He was a stout man who seemed glad to dismount and stretch, arching his back and grunting.

He smiled as he saw Duncan's hesitation. "Are you much alone here, my son?"

"Yes, Holy One. But—last night I had a sign. For two years I've wanted one, and just last night it came."

"Indeed? That is good news." The priest's eyes strayed to the mountain, and to the sun, as if he calculated how much time he could spare. But he said, with no sound of impatience: "Tell me about it, if you wish."

When he heard that the flash in the sky was Duncan's sign, the priest frowned. Then he seemed to keep himself from smiling. "My son, that light was seen by many. Today the elders of a dozen villages of most of the Tribe, have come to the Temple Village. Everyone has seen something different in the sky flash, and I am now going to pray in a cave, because of it.''

The priest remounted, but when he had looked at Duncan again, he waited to say: ''Still, I was not one of those chosen to see the sky-gods' sign; and you were. It may be a sign for you as well as for others, so do not be disappointed if it is not only for you. Be faithful in your duties, and the sign will come.'' He turned the donkey away.

Feeling small, Duncan walked slowly back to his flock. How could he have thought that a light seen over half the world was meant for one shepherd? Now his sign was gone, but his wolf remained.

In the afternoon, another figure came into sight, walking straight across the valley toward the flock from the direction of Colleen's village. Duncan tightened the belt on his woolen tunic, and combed grass from his hair with his fingers. He felt his chin, and wished his beard would really begin to grow.

He was sure the visitor was Colleen when she was still half a mile away. He kept his movements calm and made himself appear to first notice her when she came in sight on a hilltop within hailing distance. The wind moved her brown hair and her garments.

''Hello, Colleen.''

''Hello, Duncan the Herdsman. My father sent me to ask about his sheep.''

He ran an anxious eye over the flock, picking out individuals. Praise be to gods of land and sky. ''Your father's sheep are well.''

She walked closer to him. "Here are some cakes. The other sheep are not well?"

Ah, she was beautiful. But no mere herdsman would ever have her.

"Last night the wolf killed again." Duncan gestured with empty hands. "I watch, I light fires. I have a spear and a club, and I rush at him when he comes, and I drive him away. But sooner or later he comes on the wrong side of the flock, or a sheep strays."

"Another man should come from the village," she said. "Even a boy would help. With a big clever wolf, any herdsman may need help."

He nodded, faintly pleased at her implying he was a man. But his troubles were too big to be soothed away. "Did you see the sky flash, last night?" he asked, remembering with bitterness his joy when he had thought the sign was his.

"No, but all the village is talking about it. I will tell them about the wolf, but probably no man will come to help you for a day or two. They are all dancing and talking, thinking of nothing but the sky flash." She raised puzzled eyes beyond Duncan. "Look."

It was the priest, rushing past half a mile from them on his way down-Valley from the caves, doing his best to make his donkey gallop toward the Temple Village.

"He may have met your wolf," Colleen suggested.

"He doesn't look behind him. Maybe in the caves he received an important sign from the earth-gods."

They talked a while longer, sitting on the grass, while he ate the cakes she had brought him.

"I must go!" She sprang up. The sun was lowering and neither of them had realized it.

197

"Yes, hurry! At night the wolf may be anywhere on the plain."

Watching her hurry away, Duncan felt the wolf in his own blood. Perhaps she knew it, for she looked back at him strangely from the hilltop. Then she was gone.

On a hillside, gathering dried brush for the night's watchfires, Duncan paused for a moment, looking at the sunset.

"Sky-gods, help me," he prayed. "And earth-gods, the dark wolf should be under your dominion. If you will not grant me a sign, at least help me deal with the wolf." He bent routinely and laid his ear to a rock. Every day he asked some god for a sign, but never—

He heard a voice. He crouched there, listening to the rock, unable to believe. Surely it was a waterfall he heard, or running cattle somewhere near. But no, it was a real voice, booming and shouting in some buried distance. He could not make out the words, but it was a real god-voice from under the earth.

He straightened up, tears in his eyes, even the sheep for a moment forgotten. This wonderful sign was not for half the world, it was for him! And he had doubted that it would ever come.

To hear what it said was all-important. He bent again and listened. The muffled voice went on unceasingly, but he could not understand it. He ran a few steps up the hill, and put his ear against another exposed earth-bone of rock. Yes, the voice was plainer here; sometimes he could distinguish a word. "Give," said the voice. Mumble, mumble. "Defend," he thought it said. Even the words he recognized were spoken in strange accents.

He realized that darkness was falling, and stood up, in fearful indecision. The sheep were still his responsibility, and he had to light watchfires, he *had* to, for the sheep would be slaughtered without them. And at the same time he had to listen to this voice.

A form moved toward him through the twilight, and he grabbed up his club—then he realized it was Colleen.

She looked frightened. She whispered: "The sun went down, and I feared the dark. It was a shorter way back to you than on to the village."

The berserker moved in toward the nightside of the planet, quickly now, but still with caution. It had searched its memory of thousands of years of war against a thousand kinds of life, and it had remembered one other planet like this, with defensive satellites but no cities or radios. The fortifiers of that planet had fought among themselves, weakening themselves until they could no longer operate their defenses, had even forgotten what their planet-weapons were.

The life here might be shamming, trying to lure the berserker within range of the planet-weapons. Therefore the berserker sent its mechanical scouts ahead, to break through the satellite net and range over the land surface, killing, until they provoked the planet's maximum response.

The fires were built, and Colleen held the spear and watched the sheep. Wolf or not, Duncan had to follow his sign. He made his way up the dark hillside, listening at rock after rock. And ever the earth-god voice grew stronger.

In the back of his mind Duncan realized that Colleen had arranged to be trapped with him for the night, to help him defend the sheep, and he felt limitless gratitude and love. But even that was now in the back of his mind. The voice now was everything.

He held his breath, listening. Now he could hear the voice while he stood erect. There, ahead, at the foot of a cliff, were slabs of rock tumbled down by snowslides. Among them might be a cave.

He reached the slabs, and heard the voice rumble up between them. "Attack in progress. Request human response. Order one requested. This is defense control. Attack in progress—"

On and on it went. Duncan understood some of it. Attack, request, human. Order one requested—that must mean one wish was to be granted, as in the legends. Never again would Duncan laugh at legends, thinking himself wise. This was no prank of the other young men; no one could hide in a cave and shout on and on in such a voice.

No one but a priest should enter a cave, but probably not even the priests knew of this one. It was Duncan's, for his sign had led him here. He had been granted a tremendous sign.

More awed than fearful, he slid between slabs of rock, finding the way down, rock and earth and then metal under his feet. He dropped into a low metal cave, which was as he had heard the god-caves described, very long, smooth, round and regular, except here where it was bent and torn under the fallen rocks. In the cave's curving sides were glowing places, like huge animal eyes, giving light enough to see.

And here the shouting was very loud. Duncan moved toward it.

We have reached the surface, the scouts radioed back to the berserker, in their passionless computer-symbol language. *Here intelligent life of the earth-type lives in villages. So far we have killed eight hundred and thirty-nine units. We have met no response from dangerous weapons.*

A little while longer the berserker waited, letting the toll of life-units mount. When the chance of this planet's being a trap had dropped in computer-estimation to the vanishing point, the berserker moved in to close range, and began to mop the remaining defensive satellites out of its way.

"Here I am." Duncan fell on his knees before the metal thing that bellowed. In front of the god-shape lay woven twigs and eggshells, very old. Once priests had sacrificed here, and then they had forgotten this god.

"Here I am," said Duncan again, in a louder voice.

The god heeded him, for the deafening shouting stopped.

"Response acknowledged, from defense control alternate 9,864," said the god. "Planetary defenses now under control of post 9,864."

How could you ask a god to speak more plainly?

After a very short time of silence, the god said: "Request order one."

That seemed understandable, but to make sure, Duncan asked: "You will grant me one wish, mighty one?"

"Will obey your order. Emergency. Satellite sphere ninety percent destroyed. Planet-weapon responses fully programmed, activation command requested."

Duncan, still kneeling, closed his eyes. One wish would be granted him. The rest of the words he took as a warning to choose his wish with care. If he wished, the gods would make him the wisest of chiefs or the bravest of warriors. The god would give him a hundred years of life or a dozen young wives.

Or Colleen.

But Colleen was out in the darkness, now, facing the wolf. Even now the wolf might be prowling near, just beyond the circle of firelight, watching the sheep, and watching the tender girl. Even now Colleen might be screaming—

Duncan's heart sank utterly, for he knew the wolf had beaten him, had destroyed this moment on which the rest of his life depended. He was still a herdsman. And if he could make himself forget the sheep, he would not want to forget Colleen.

"Destroy the wolf! Kill it!" he choked out.

"Term wolf questioned."

"The killer! To destroy the killer! That is the only wish I can make!" He could stand the presence of the god no longer, and ran away through the cave, weeping for his ruined life. He ran to find Colleen.

Recall, shouted the electronic voice of the berserker. *Trap. Recall.*

Hearing, its scattered brood of scout machines rose at top acceleration from their planet work, curving and climbing toward their great metal mother. Too slow. They blurred into streaks, into fireworks of incandescent gas.

The berserker was not waiting for them. It was diving for deep-space, knowing the planet-weapons reached out for it. It wasted no circuits now trying to compute why so much life had been sacrificed to trap it. Then it saw new force fields thrown up ahead of it, walling it in. No escape.

The whole sky was in flames, the bones of the hills shuddered underfoot, and at the head of the valley the top of the mountain was torn away and an enormous shaft of something almost invisible poured from it infinitely up into the sky.

Duncan saw Colleen huddling on the open ground, shouting to him, but the buried thunder drowned her voice. The sheep were running and leaping, crying under the terrible sky. Duncan saw the dark wolf among them, running with them in circles, too frightened to be a wolf. He picked up his club and ran, staggering with the shaking earth, after the beast.

He caught the wolf, for he ran toward it, while it ran in circles without regard for him. He saw the sky reflected in its eyes, facing him, and he swung his club just as it crouched to leap.

He won. And then he struck again and again, making sure.

All at once there was a blue-white, moving sun in the sky, a marvelous sun that in a minute turned red, and spread itself out to vanish in the general glow. Then the earth was still at last.

Duncan walked in a daze, until he saw Colleen trying to round up the sheep. Then he waved to her, and trotted after her to help. The wolf was dead, and he had a wonderful sign to tell. The gods had not killed him. Beneath his running feet, the steadiness of the ground seemed permanent.

I have seen, and I still see, a future in which you, the Earth-descended, may prevail over the wolves of planets and the wolves of space. For at every stage of your civilizations there are numbers of you who put aside selfishness and dedicate their lives in service to something they see as being greater than themselves.

I say you may prevail, I say not that you will. For in each of your generations there are men who choose to serve the gods of darkness.

IN THE TEMPLE OF MARS

SOMETHING WAS DRIVING waves of confusion through his mind, so that he knew not who he was, or where. How long ago what was happening had started or what had gone before it he could not guess. Nor could he resist what was happening, or even decide if he wanted to resist.

A chant beat on his ears, growled out by barbaric voices:

On the wall there was painted a forest
In which there lived neither man nor beast
With knotty, gnarled, barren trees, old . . .

And he could see the forest around him. Whether the trees and the chanting voices were real or not was a question he could not even formulate, with the confusion patterns racking his mind.

Through broken branches hideous to behold
There ran a cold and sighing sind
As if a storm would break down every bough

And downward, at the bottom of a hill
Stood the temple of Mars who is mighty in arms . . .

And he saw the temple. It was of steel, curved in the dread shape of a berserker's hull, and half-sunken in dark earth. At the entrance, gates of steel sang and shuddered in the cold wind rushing out of the temple, rushing out endlessly to rage through the shattered forest. The whole scene was gray, and lighted from above by an auroral flickering.

The northern lights shone in at the doors
For there was no window on the walls
Through which men might any light discern . . .

He seemed to pass, with a conqueror's strides, between the clawlike gates, toward the temple door.

The door was of eternal adamant
Bound lengthways and sideways with tough iron
And to make the temple stronger, every pillar
Was thick as a barrel, of iron bright and shiny.

The inside of the temple was a kaleidoscope of violence, a frantic abattoir. Hordes of phantasmal men were mowed down in scenes of war, women were slaughtered by machines, children crushed and devoured by animals. He, the conqueror, accepted it all, exulted in it all, even as he became aware that his mind, under some outer compulsion, was building it all from the words of the chant.

He could not tell how long it lasted. The end came abruptly—the pressure on his mind was eased, and the chanting stopped. The relief was such that he fell sprawling, his eyes closed, a soft surface beneath him. Except for his own breathing, all was quiet.

A gentle thud made him open his eyes. A short metal sword had been dropped or tossed from somewhere to land near him. He was in a round, softly lighted, familiar room. The circular wall was covered by a continuous mural, depicting a thousand variations on the theme of bloody violence. At one side of the room, behind a low altar, toward the statue of an armed man gripping chariot reins and battleax, a man who was larger than life and more than a man, his bronze face a mask of insensate rage.

All this he had seen before. He gave it little thought except for the sword. He was drawn to the sword like a steel particle to a magnet, for the power of his recent vision was still fresh and irresistible, and it was the power of destruction. He crawled to the sword, noticing dimly that he was dressed like the statue of the god, in a coat of mail. When he had the sword in his hand the power of it drew him to his feet. He looked round expectantly.

A section of the continuous mural-wall opened into a door, and a figure entered the temple. It was dressed in a neat, plain uniform, and its face was lean and severe. It looked like a man, but it was not a man, for no blood gushed out when the sword hewed in.

Joyfully, thoughtlessly, he hacked the plastic-bodied figure into a dozen pieces. Then he stood swaying over it, drained and weary. The metal pommel of the sword grew suddenly hot in his hand, so that he had to drop it. All this had happened before, again and again.

This painted door opened once more. This time it was a real man who entered, a man dressed in black, who had hypnotic eyes under bushy brows.

"Tell me your name," the black-uniform ordered. His voice compelled.

"My name is Jor."

"And mine?"

"You are Katsulos," said Jor dully, "the Esteeler secret police."

"Yes. And where are we?"

"In space, aboard the *Nirvana II*. We are taking the High Lord Nogara's new space-going castle out to him, out to the rim of the galaxy. And when he comes aboard, I am supposed to entertain him by killing someone with a sword. Or another gladiator will entertain him by killing me."

"Normal bitterness," remarked one of Katsulos' men, appearing in the doorway behind him.

"Yes, this one always snaps right back," Katsulos said. "But a good subject. See the brain rhythms?" He showed the other a torn-off piece of chart from some recording device.

They stood there discussing Jor like a specimen, while he waited and listened. They had taught Jor to behave. They thought they had taught him permanently—but one of these days he was going to show them. Before it was too late. He shivered in his mail coat.

"Take him back to his cell," Katsulos ordered at last. "I'll be along in a moment."

Jor looked about him confusedly as he was led out of the temple and down some stairs. His recollection of the treament he had just undergone was already becoming uncertain; and what he did remember was so unpleasant that he made no effort to recall more. But his sullen determination to strike back stayed with him, stronger than ever. He had to strike back, somehow, and soon.

Left alone in the temple, Katsulos kicked the pieces

of the plastic dummy into a pile, to be ready for careful salvage. He trod heavily on the malleable face, making it unrecognizable, just in case someone beside his own men should happen to see it.

Then he stood for a moment looking up into the maniacal bronze face of Mars. And Katsulos' eyes, that were cold weapons when he turned them on other men, were now alive.

A communicator sounded, in what was to be the High Lord Nogara's cabin when he took delivery of *Nirvana II*. Admiral Hemphill, alone in the cabin, needed a moment to find the proper switch on the huge, unfamiliar desk. "What is it?"

"Sir, our rendezvous with the Solarian courier is completed; we're ready to drive again, unless you have any last-minute messages to transmit?"

"Negative. Our new passenger came aboard?"

"Yes, sir. A Solarian, named Mitchell Spain, as we were advised."

"I know the man, Captain. Will you ask him to come to this cabin as soon as possible? I'd like to talk to him at once."

"Yes sir."

"Are those police still snooping around the bridge?"

"Not at the moment, Admiral."

Hemphill shut off the communicator and leaned back in the thronelike chair from which Felipe Nogara would soon survey his Esteeler empire; but soon the habitually severe expression of Hemphill's lean face deepened and he stood up. The luxury of this cabin did not please him.

On the blouse of Hemphill's neat, plain uniform were seven ribbons of scarlet and black, each representing a battle in which one or more berserker machines had been destroyed. He wore no other decorations except his insignia of rank, granted him by the United Planets, the anti-berserker league, of which all worlds were at least nominal members.

Within a minute the cabin door opened. The man who entered, dressed in civilian clothes, was short and muscular and rather ugly. He smiled at once, and came toward Hemphill, saying: "So it's High Admiral Hemphill now. Congratulations. It's a long time since we've met."

"Thank you. Yes, not since the Stone Place." Hemphill's mouth bent upward slightly at the corners, and he moved around the desk to shake hands. "You were a captain of marines, then, as I recall."

As they gripped hands, both men thought back to that day of victory. Neither of them could smile at it now, for the war was going badly again.

"Yes, that's nine years ago," said Mitchell Spain. "Now—I'm a foreign correspondent for Solar News Service. They're sending me out to interview Nogara."

"I've heard that you've made a reputation as a writer." Hemphill motioned Mitch to a chair. "I'm afraid I have no time myself for literature or other nonessentials."

Mitch sat down, and dug out his pipe. He knew Hemphill well enough to be sure that no slur was intended by the reference to literature. To Hemphill, everything was nonessential except the destruction of berserker machines; and today such a viewpoint was doubtless a good one for a High Admiral.

Mitch got the impression that Hemphill had serious business to talk about, but was uncertain of how to broach the subject. To fill the hesitant silence, Mitch remarked: "I wonder if the High Lord Nogara will be pleased with his new ship." He gestured around the cabin with the stem of his pipe.

Everything was as quiet and steady as if rooted on the surface of a planet. There was nothing to suggest that even now the most powerful engines ever built by Earth-descended man were hurling this ship out toward the rim of the galaxy at many times the speed of light.

Hemphill took the remark as a cue. Leaning slightly forward in his uncomfortable-looking seat, he said: "I'm not concerned about his liking it. What concerns me is how it's going to be used."

Since the Stone Place, Mitch's left hand was mostly scar tissue and prosthetics. He used one plastic finger now to tamp down the glowing coal of his pipe. "You mean Nogara's idea of shipboard fun? I caught a glimpse just now of the gladitorial arena. I've never met him, but they say he's gone bad, really bad, since Karlsen's death."

"I wasn't talking about Nogara's so-called amusements. What I'm really getting at is this: Johann Karlsen may be still alive."

Hemphill's calm, fantastic statement hung in the quiet cabin air. For a moment Mitch thought that he could sense the motion of the C-plus ship as it traversed spaces no man understood, spaces where it seemed time could mean nothing and the dead of all the ages might still be walking.

Mitch shook his head. "Are we talking about the same Johann Karlsen?"

"Of course."

"Two years ago he went down into a hypermassive

sun, with a berserker-controlled ship on his tail. Unless that story's not true?''

"It's perfectly true, except we think now that his launch went into orbit around the hypermass instead of falling into it. Have you seen the girl who's aboard?''

"I passed a girl, outside your cabin here. I thought . . .''

"No, I have no time for that. Her name is Lucinda, single names are the custom on her planet. She's an eyewitness of Karlsen's vanishing.''

"Oh. Yes, I remember the story. But what's this about his being in orbit?''

Hemphill stood up and seemed to become more comfortable, as another man would be sitting down. "Ordinarily, the hypermass and everything near it is invisible, due to the extreme red shift caused by its gravity. But during the last year some scientists have done their best to study it. Their ship didn't compare to this one''—Hemphill turned his head for a moment, as if he could hear the mighty engines—''but they went as close as they dared, carrying some new instruments, long-wave telescopes. The star itself was still invisible, but they brought back these.''

Hemphill stood behind him. "That's what space looks like near the hypermass. Remember, it has about a billion times the mass of Sol, packed into roughly the same volume. Gravity like that does things we don't yet understand.''

"Interesting. What forms these dark lines?''

"Falling dust that's become trapped in lines of gravitic force, like the lines round a magnet. Or so I'm told.''

"And where's Karlsen supposed to be?''

Hemphill's finger descended on a photo, pointing

out a spot of crystalline roundness, tiny as a raindrop within a magnified line of dust. "We think this is his launch. Its orbiting about a hundred million miles from the center of the hypermass. And the berserker-controlled ship that was chasing him is here, following him in the same dust-line. Now they're both stuck. No ordinary engines can drive a ship down there."

Mitch stared at the photos, looking past them into old memories that came flooding back. "And you think he's alive."

"He had equipment that would let him freeze himself into suspended animation. Also, time may be running quite slowly for him. He's in a three-hour orbit."

"A three-hour orbit, at a hundred million miles . . . wait a minute."

Hemphill almost smiled. "I told you, things we don't understand yet."

"All right." Mitch nodded slowly. "So you think there's a chance? He's not a man to give up. He'd fight as long as he could, and then invent a way to fight some more."

"Yes, I think there is a chance." Hemphill's face had become iron again. "You saw what efforts the berserkers made to kill him. They feared him, in their iron guts, as they feared no one else. Though I never quite understood why . . . So, if we can save him, we must do so without delay. Do you agree?"

"Certainly, but how?"

"With this ship. It has the strongest engines ever built—trust Nogara to have seen to that, with his own safety in mind."

Mitch whistled softly. "Strong enough to match orbits with Karlsen and pull him out of there?"

"Yes, mathematically. Supposedly."

"And you mean to make the attempt before this ship is delivered to Nogara."

"Afterwards may be too late; you know he wanted Karlsen out of the way. With these police aboard I've been keeping my rescue plan a secret."

Mitch nodded. He felt a rising excitement. "Nogara may rage if we save Karlsen, but they'll be nothing he can do. How about the crew, are they willing?"

"I've already sounded out the captain; he's with me. And since I hold my admiral's rank from the United Planets I can issue legal orders on any ship, if I say I'm acting against berserkers." Hemphill began to pace. "The only thing that worries me is this detachment of Nogara's police we have aboard; they're certain to oppose the rescue."

"How many of them are there?"

"A couple of dozen. I don't know why there are so many, but they outnumber the rest of us two to one. Not counting their prisoners, who of course are helpless."

"Prisoners?"

"About forty young men, I understand. Sword fodder for the arena."

Lucinda spent a good deal of her time wandering, restless and alone, through the corridors of the great ship. Today she happened to be in a passage not far from the central bridge and flag quarters when a door opened close ahead of her and three men came into view. The two who wore black uniforms held a single prisoner, clad in a shirt of chain mail, between them.

When she saw the black uniforms, Lucinda's chin lifted. She waited, standing in their path.

"Go round me, vultures," she said in an icy voice

when they came up to her. She did not look at the prisoner; bitter experience had taught her that showing sympathy for Nogara's victims could bring added suffering upon them.

The black uniforms halted in front of her. "I am Katsulos," said the bushy-browed one. "Who are you?"

"Once my planet was Flamland," she said, and from the corner of her eye she saw the prisoner's face turn up. "One day it will be my home again, when it is freed of Nogara's vultures."

The second black uniform opened his mouth to reply, but never got out a word, for just then the prisoner's elbow came smashing back into his belly. Then the prisoner, who till now had stood meek as a lamb, shoved Katsulos off his feet and was out of sight around a bend of corridor before either policeman could recover.

Katsulos bounced quickly to his feet. His gun drawn, he pushed past Lucinda to the bend of the corridor. Then she saw his shoulders slump.

Her delighted laughter did not seem to sting Katsulos in the least.

"There's nowhere he can go," he said. The look in his eyes choked off her laughter in her throat.

Katsulos posted police guards on the bridge and in the engine room, and secured all lifeboats. "The man Jor is desperate and dangerous," he explained to Hemphill and to Mitchell Spain. "Half of my men are searching for him continuously, but you know how big this ship is. I ask you to stay close to your quarters until he's caught."

A day passed, and Jor was not caught. Mitch took

advantage of the police dispersal to investigae th·: arena—Solar News would be much interested.

He climbed a short stair and emerged squirming in imitation sunlight, under a high-domed ceiling as blue as Earth's sky. He found himself behind the upper row of the approximately two hundred seats that encircled the arena behind a sloping crystalline wall. At the bottom of the glassy bowl, the oval-shaped fighting area was about thirty yards long. It was floored by a substance that looked like sand but was doubtless something more cohesive, that would not fly up in a cloud if the artificial gravity chanced to fail.

In this facility as slickly modern as a death-ray the worst vices of ancient Rome could be most efficiently enjoyed. Every spectator would be able to see every drop of blood. There was only one awkward-looking feature: set at equal intervals around the upper rim of the arena, behind the seats, were three buildings, each as large as a small house. Their architecture seemed to Mitch to belong somewhere on Ancient Earth, not here; their purpose was not immediately apparent.

Mitch took out his pocket camera and made a few photographs from where he stood. Then he walked behind the rows of seats to the nearest of the buildings. A door stood open, and he went in.

At first he thought he had discovered an entrance to Nogara's private harem; but after a moment he saw that the people in the paintings covering the walls were not all, or even most of them, engaged in sexual embraces. There were men and women and godlike beings, posed in a variety of relationships, in the costumes of Ancient Earth when they wore any costumes at all. As Mitch snapped a few more photos he gradually realized that each painted scene was meant to depict some aspect of human love. It was puzzling. He had not expected to find love here, or in any part of Felipe Nogara's chosen environment.

As he left the temple through another door, he passed a smiling statue, evidently the resident goddess. She was bronze, and the upper part of her beautiful body emerged nude from glittering sea-green waves. He photographed her and moved on.

The second building's interior paintings showed scenes of hunting and of women in childbirth. The goddess of this temple was clothed modestly in bright green, and armed with a bow and quiver. Bronze hounds waited at her feet, eager for the chase.

As he moved on to the last temple, Mitch found his steps quickening slightly. He had the feeling that something was drawing him on.

Whatever attraction might have existed was annihilated in revulsion as soon as he stepped into the place. If the first building was a temple raised to love, surely this one honored hate.

On the painted wall opposite the entrance, a sowlike beast thrust its ugly head into a cradle, devouring the screaming child. Beside it, men in togas, faces glowing with hate, stabbed one of their number to death. All around the walls men and women and children suffered pointlessly and died horribly, without hope. The spirit of destruction was almost palpable within this room. It was like a berserker's—

Mitch took a step back and closed his eyes, bracing his arms against the sides of the entrance. Yes, he could feel it. Something more than painting and lighting had been set to work here, to honor Hate. Something physical, that Mitch found not entirely unfamiliar.

Years ago, during a space battle, he had experienced

the attack of a berserker's mind beam. Men had learned how to shield their ships from mind beams—did they now bring the enemy's weapons inside deliberately?

Mitch opened his eyes. The radiation he felt now was very weak, but it carried something worse than mere confusion.

He stepped back and forth through the entrance. Outside the thick walls of the temple, thicker than those of the other buildings, the effect practically disappeared. Inside, it was definitely perceptible, an energy that pricked at the rage centers of the brain. Slowly, slowly, it seemed to be fading, like a residual charge from a machine that had been turned off. If he could feel it now, what must this temple be like when the projector was on?

More importantly, why was such a thing here at all? Only to goad a few gladiators on to livelier deaths? Possibly. Mitch glanced at this temple's towering bronze god, riding his chariot over the world, and shivered. He suspected something worse than the simple brutality of Roman games.

He took a few more pictures, and then remembered seeing an intercom station near the first temple he had entered. He walked back there, and punched out the number of Ship's Records on the intercom keys.

When the automated voice answered, he ordered: "I want some information about the design of this arena, particularly the three structures spaced around the upper rim."

The voice asked if he wanted diagrams.

"No. At least not yet. Just tell me what you can about the designer's basic plan."

There was a delay of several seconds. Then the voice

said: "The basic designer was a man named Oliver Mical, since deceased. In his design programming, frequent reference is made to descriptive passages within a literary work by one Geoffrey Chaucer of Ancient Earth. The quote fantastic unquote work is titled The Knight's Tale."

The name of Chaucer rang only the faintest of bells for Mitch. But he remembered that Oliver Mical had been one of Nogara's brainwashing experts, and also a classical scholar.

"What kind of psychoelectronic devices are built into these three structures?"

"There is no record aboard of any such installation."

Mitch was sure about the hate-projector. It might have been built in secretly; it probably *had* been, if his worst suspicions were true.

He ordered: "Read me some of the relevant passages of this literary work."

"The three temples are those of Mars, Diana, and Venus," said the intercom. "A passage relevant to the temple of Mars follows, in original language:

"First on the wal was peynted a forest
In which there dwelleth neither man ne beast
With knotty, knarry, barreyn trees olde
Of stubbes sharp and hidous to biholde."

Mitch knew just enough of ancient languages to catch a word here and there, but he was not really listening now. His mind had stopped on that phrase "temple of Mars." He had heard it before, recently, applied to a newly risen secret cult of berserker-worshippers.

"And downward from a hill, under a bente

Ther stood the temple of Mars armipotente
Wrought all of burned steel, of which the entree
Was long and streit, and gastly for to see."

There was a soft sound behind Mitch, and he turned
quickly. Katsulos stood there. He was smiling, but his
eyes reminded Mitch of Mars' statue.

"Do you understand the ancient language, Spain?
No? Then I shall translate." He took up the verse in a
chanting voice:

"Then saw I first the dark imagining
Of felony, and all its compassing
The cruel ire, red as any fire
The pickpurse, and also the pale dread
The smiler with the knife under his cloak
The stable burning with the black smoke
The treason of the murdering in the bed
The open war, with all the wounds that bled . . ."

"Who are you, really?" Mitch demanded. He
wanted it out in the open. And he wanted to gain time,
for Katsulos wore a pistol at his belt. "What is this to
you? Some kind of religion?"

"Not *some* religion!" Katsulos shook his head,
while his eyes glowed steadily at Mitch. "Not a
mythology of distant gods, not a system of pale ethics
for dusty philosophers. No!" He took a step closer.
"Spain, there is no time now for me to proselyte with
craft and subtlety. I say only this—the temple of Mars
stands open to you. The new god of all creation will
accept your sacrifice and your love."

"You pray to that bronze statue?" Mitch shifted his
weight slightly, getting ready.

"No!" The fanatic's words poured out faster and
louder. "The figure with helmet and sword is our

symbol and no more. Our god is new, and real, and worthy. He wields deathbeam and missile, and his glory is as the nova sun. He is the descendant of Life, and feeds on Life as is his right. And we who give ourselves to any of his units become immortal in him, though our flesh perish at his touch!''

"I've heard there were men who prayed to berserkers,'' said Mitch. "Somehow I never expected to meet one.'' Faintly in the distance he heard a man shouting, and feet pounding down a corridor. Suddenly he wondered if he, or Katsulos, was more likely to receive reinforcement.

"Soon we will be everywhere,'' said Katsulos loudly. "We are here now, and we are seizing this ship. We will use it to save the unit of our god orbiting the hypermass. And we will give the badlife Karlsen to Mars, and we will give ourselves. And through Mars we will live forever!''

He looked into Mitch's face and started to draw his gun, just as Mitch hurled himself forward.

Katsulos tried to spin away, Mitch failed to get a solid grip on him, and both men fell sprawling. Mitch saw the gun muzzle swing round on him, and dived desperately for shelter behind a row of seats. Splinters flew around him as the gun blasted. In an instant he was moving again, in a crouching run that carried him into the temple of Venus by one door and out by another. Before Katsulos could sight at him for another shot, Mitch had leaped down an exit stairway, out of the arena.

As he emerged into a corridor, he heard gunfire from the direction of the crew's quarters. He went the other way, heading for Hemphill's cabin. At a turn in the passage a black uniform stepped out to bar his way, aiming a pistol. Mitch charged without hesitation, taking the policeman by surprise. The gun fired as Mitch knocked it aside, and then his rush bowled the black-uniform over. Mitch sat on the man and clobbered him with fists and elbows until he was quiet.

Then, captured gun in hand, Mitch hurried on to Hemphill's door. It slid open before he could pound on it, and closed again as soon as he had jumped inside.

A dead black-uniform sat leaning against the wall, unseeing eyes aimed at Mitch, bullet-holes patterned across his chest.

"Welcome," said Hemphill drily. He stood with his left hand on an elaborate control console that had been raised from a place of concealment inside the huge desk. In his right hand a machine pistol hung casually. "It seems we face greater difficulties than we expected."

Lucinda sat in the darkened cabin that was Jor's hiding place, watching him eat. Immediately after his escape she had started roaming the ship's passages, looking for him, whispering his name, until at last he had answered her. Since then she had been smuggling him food and drink.

He was older than she had thought at first glance; a man of about her own age, with tiny lines at the corners of his suspicious eyes. Paradoxically, the more she helped him, the more suspicious his eyes became.

Now he paused in his eating to ask: "What do you plan to do when we reach Nogara, and a hundred men come aboard to search for me? They'll soon find me, then."

She wanted to tell Jor about Hemphill's plan for

222

rescuing Karlsen. Once Johann Karlsen was aboard, no one on this ship would have to fear Nogara, or so she felt. But just because Jor still seemed suspicious of her, she hesitated to trust him with a secret.

"You knew you'd be caught eventually," she countered. "So why did you run away?"

"You don't know what it's like, being their prisoner."

"I do know."

He ignored her contradiction. "They trained me to fight in the arena with the others. And then they singled me out, and began to train me for something even worse. Now they flick a switch somewhere, and I start to kill, like a berserker."

"What do you mean?"

He closed his eyes, his food forgotten. "I think there's a man they want me to assassinate. Every day or so they put me in the temple of Mars and drive me mad, and then the image of this man is always sent to me. Always it's the same face and uniform. And I must destroy the image, with a sword or a gun or with my hands. I have no choice when they flip that switch, no control over myself. They've hollowed me out and filled me up with their own madness. They're madmen. I think they go into the temple themselves, and turn the foul madness on, and wallow in it, before their idol."

He had never said so much to her in one speech before. She was not sure how much of it was true, but she felt he believed it all. She reached for his hand.

"Jor, I do know something about them. That's why I've helped you. And I've seen other men who were really brainwashed. They haven't really destroyed you, you'll be all right again someday."

"They want me to look normal." He opened his

eyes, which were still suspicious. "Why are you on this ship, anyway?"

"Because." She looked into the past. "Two years ago I met a man called Johann Karlsen. Yes, the one everyone knows of. I spent about ten minutes with him . . . if he's still alive, he's certainly forgotten me, but I fell in love with him."

"In love!" Jor snorted, and began to pick his teeth.

Or I thought I fell in love, she said to herself. Watching Jor now, understanding and forgiving his sullen mistrust, she realized she was no longer able to visualize Karlsen's face clearly.

Something triggered Jor's taut nerves, and he jumped up to peek out of the cabin into the passage. "What's that noise? Hear? It sounds like fighting."

"So." Hemphill's voice was grimmer than usual. "The surviving crewmen are barricaded in their quarters, surrounded and under attack. The damned berserker-lovers hold the bridge, and the engine room. In fact they hold the ship, except for this." He patted the console that he had raised from concealment inside Nogara's innocent-looking desk. "I know Felipe Nogara, and I thought he'd have a master control in his cabin, and when I saw all the police I thought I might possibly need it. That's why I quartered myself in here."

"What all does it control?" Mitch asked, wiping his hands. He had just dragged the dead man into a closet. Katsulos should have known better than to send only one against the High Admiral.

"I believe it will override any control on the bridge or in the engine room. With it I can open or close most of the doors and hatches on the ship. And there seem to be scanners hidden in a hundred places, connected to this little viewscreen. The berserker-lovers aren't going anywhere with this ship until they've done a lot of rewiring or gotten us out of this cabin.''

"I don't suppose we're going anywhere either,'' said Mitch. "Have you any idea what's happened to Lucy?''

"No. She and that man Jor may be free, and they may do us some good, but we can't count on it. Spain, look here.'' Hemphill pointed to the little screen. "This is a view inside the guardroom and prison, under the arena's seats. If all those individual cells are occupied, there must be about forty men in there.''

"That's an idea. They may be trained fighters, and they'll certainly have no love for the black uniforms.''

"I could talk to them from here,'' Hemphill mused. "But how can we free them and arm them? I can't control their individual cell doors, though I can keep the enemy locked out of that area, at least for a while. Tell me, how did the fighting start? What set it off?''

Mitch told Hemphill what he knew. "It's almost funny. The cultists have the same idea you have, of taking this ship out to the hypermass and going after Karlsen. Only of course they want to give him to the berserkers.'' He shook his head. "I suppose Katsulos hand-picked cultists from among the police for this mission. There must be more of them around than any of us thought.''

Hemphill only shrugged. Maybe he understood fairly well those fanatics out there whose polarity happened to be opposite from his own.

Lucinda would not leave Jor now, nor let him leave her. Like hunted animals they made their way through the corridors, which she knew well from her days of restless walking. She guided him around the sounds of fighting to where he wanted to go.

He peered around the last corner, and brought his head back to whisper: "There's no one at the guard-room door."

"But how will you get in? And some of the vultures may be inside, and you're not armed."

He laughed soundlessly. "What have I to lose? My *life?*" He moved on around the corner.

Mitch's fingers suddenly dug into Hemphill's arm. "Look! Jor's there, with the same idea you had. Open the door for him, quick!"

Most of the painted panels had been removed from the interior walls of the temple of Mars. Two black-uniformed men were at work upon the mechanism thus revealed, while Katsulos sat at the altar, watching Jor's progress through his own secret scanners. When he saw Jor and Lucinda being let into the guardroom, Katsulos pounced.

"Quick, turn on the beam and focus on him. Boil his brain with it! He'll kill everyone in there, and then we can take our time with the others."

Katsulos' two assistants hurried to obey, arranging cables and a directional antenna. One asked: "He's the one you were training to assassinate Hemphill?"

"Yes. His brain rhythms are on the chart. Focus on him quickly!"

"Set them free and arm them!" Hemphill's image shouted, from a guardroom viewscreen. "You men there! Fight with us and I promise to take you to freedom when the ship is ours; and I promise we'll take Johann Karlsen with us, if he's alive.''

There was a roar from the cells at the offer of freedom, and another roar at Karlsen's name. "With him, we'd go on to Esteel itself!'' one prisoner shouted.

When the beam from the temple of Mars struck downward, it went unfelt by everyone but Jor. The others in the guardroom had not been conditioned by repeated treatments, and the heat of their emotions was already high.

Just as Jor picked up the keys that would open the cells, the beam hit him. He knew what was happening, but there was nothing he could do about it. In a paroxysm of rage he dropped the keys, and grabbed an automatic weapon from the arms rack. He fired at once, shattering Hemphill's image from the viewscreen.

With the fragment of his mind that was still his own, Jor felt despair like that of a drowning man. He knew he was not going to be able to resist what was coming next.

When Jor fired at the viewscreen, Lucinda understood what was being done to him.

"Jor, no!'' She fell to her knees before him. The face of Mars looked down at her, frightening beyond anything she had ever seen. But she cried out to Mars: "Jor, stop! I love you!''

Mars laughed at her love, or tried to laugh. But Mars could not quite manage to point the weapon at her. Jor was trying to come back into his own face again, now coming back halfway, struggling terribly.

"And you love me, Jor. I know. Even if they force you to kill me, remember I know that.''

Jor, clinging to his fragment of sanity, felt a healing

power come to him, setting itself against the power of Mars. In his mind danced the pictures he had once glimpsed inside the temple of Venus. Of course! There must be a countering projector built in there, and someone had managed to turn it on.

He made the finest effort he could imagine. And then, with Lucinda before him, he made a finer effort still.

He came above his red rage like a swimmer surfacing, lungs bursting, from a drowning sea. He looked down at his hands, at the gun they held. He forced his fingers to begin opening. Mars still shouted at him, louder and louder, but Venus' power grew stronger still. His hands opened and the weapon fell.

Once the gladiators had been freed and armed the fight was soon over, though not one of the cultists even tried to surrender. Katsulos and the two with him fought to the last from inside the temple of Mars, with the hate projector at maximum power, and the recorded chanting voices roaring out their song. Perhaps Katsulos still hoped to drive his enemies to acts of self-destructive rage, or perhaps he had the projector on as an act of worship.

Whatever his reasons, the three inside the temple abosorbed the full effect themselves. Mitch had seen bad things before, but when he at last broke open the temple door, he had to turn away for a moment.

Hemphill showed only satisfaction at seeing how the worship of Mars had culminated aboard *Nirvana II*. "Let's see to the bridge and the engine room first. Then we can get this mess cleaned up and be on our way."

Mitch was glad to follow, but he was detained for a moment by Jor.

"Was it you who managed to turn on the counter-projector? If it was, I owe you much more than my life."

Mitch looked at him blankly. "Counter-projector? What're you talking about?"

"But there must be . . ."

When the others had hurried away, Jor remained in the arena, looking in awe at the thin walls of the temple of Venus, where no projector could be hidden. Then a girl's voice called, and Jor too hurried out.

There was a half minute of silence in the arena.

"Emergency condition concluded," said the voice of the intercom station, to the rows of empty seats. "Ship's records returning to normal operation. Last question asked concerned basis of temple designs. Chaucer's verse relevant to temple of Venus follows, in original language:

"I recche nat if it may bettre be
To have victorie of them, or they of me
So that I have myne lady in myne armes.
For though so be that Mars is god of Armes,
Your vertu is so great in hevene above
That, if yow list, I shall wel have my love . . ."

Venus smiled, half-risen from her glittering waves.

Men always project their beliefs and their emotions into their vision of the world. Machines can be made to see in a wider spectrum, to detect every wavelength precisely as it is, undistorted by love or hate or awe.

But still men's eyes see more than lenses do.

THE FACE OF THE DEEP

AFTER FIVE MINUTES had gone by with no apparent change in his situation, Karlsen realized that he might be going to live for a while yet. And as soon as this happened, as soon as his mind dared open its eyes again, so to speak, he began to see the depths of space around him and what they held.

There followed a short time during which he seemed unable to move; a few minutes passed while he thought he might go mad.

He rode in a crystalline bubble of a launch about twelve feet in diameter. The fortunes of war had dropped him here, halfway down the steepest gravitational hill in the known universe.

At the unseeable bottom of this hill lay a sun so massive that not a quantum of light could escape it with a visible wavelength. In less than a minute he and his raindrop of a boat had fallen here, some unmeasurable distance out of normal space, trying to escape an enemy. Karlsen had spent that falling minute in prayer, achieving something like calm, considering himself already dead.

But after that minute he was suddenly no longer falling. He seemed to have entered an orbit—an orbit that no man had ever traveled before, amid sights no eyes had ever seen.

He rode above a thunderstorm at war with a sunset—a ceaseless, soundless turmoil of fantastic clouds that filled half the sky like a nearby planet. But this cloud-mass was immeasurably bigger than any planet, vaster even than most giant stars. Its core and its cause was a hypermassive sun a billion times the weight of Sol.

The clouds were interstellar dust swept up by the pull of the hypermass; as they fell they built up electrical static which was discharged in almost continuous lightning. Karlsen saw as blue-white the nearer flashes, and those ahead of him as he rode. But most of the flashes, like most of the clouds, were far below him, and so most of his light was sullen red, wearied by climbing just a section of this gravity cliff.

Karlsen's little bubble-ship had artificial gravity of its own, and kept turning itself so its deck was down, so Karlsen saw the red light below him through the translucent deck, flaring up between his space-booted feet. He sat in the one massive chair which was fixed in the center of the bubble, and which contained the boat's controls and life-support machinery. Below the deck were one or two other opaque objects, one of these a small but powerful space-warping engine. All else around Karlsen was clear glass, holding in air, holding out radiation, but leaving his eyes and soul naked to the deeps of space around him.

When he had recovered himself enough to move

again, he took a full breath and tried his engine, tried to lift himself up out of here. As he had expected, full drive did nothing at all. He might as well have been working bicycle pedals.

Even a slight change in his orbit would have been immediately visible, for his bubble was somehow locked in position within a narrow belt of rocks and dust that stretched like a thread to girdle the vastness below him. Before the thread could bend perceptibly on its great circle it lost its identity in distance, merging with other threads into a thicker strand. This in turn was braided with other strands into a heavier belt, and so on, order above order of size, until at last (a hundred thousand miles ahead? a million?) the first bending of the great ring-pattern was perceptible; and then the arc, rainbow-colored at that point by lightning, deepened swiftly, plunging out of sight below the terrible horizon of the hypermass's shroud of dust. The fantastic cloud-shapes of that horizon, which Karlsen knew must be millions of miles away, grew closer while he looked at them. Such was the speed of his orbit.

His orbit, he guessed, must be roughly the size of Earth's path around Sol. But judging by the rate at which the surface of clouds was turning beneath him, he would complete a full circuit every fifteen minutes or so. This was madness, to out-speed light in normal space—but then, of course, space was not really normal here. It could not be. These insane orbiting threads of dust and rock suggested that here gravity had formed itself into lines of force, like magnetism.

The orbiting threads of debris above Karlsen's traveled less rapidly than his. In the nearer threads below him, he could distinguish individual rocks, passing him up like the teeth of a buzzsaw. His mind recoiled from those teeth, from the sheer grandeur of speed and distance and size.

He sat in his chair looking up at the stars. Distantly he wondered if he might be growing younger, moving backward in the time of the universe from which he had fallen . . . he was no professional mathematician or physicist, but he thought not. That was one trick the universe could not pull, even here. But the chances were that in this orbit he was aging quite slowly compared with the rest of the human race.

He realized that he was still huddling in his chair like an awed child, his fingers inside their gauntlets cramping painfully with the strength of his grip on the chair arms. He forced himself to try to relax, to begin thinking of routine matters. He had survived worse things than this display of nature, if none more awful.

He had air and water and food enough, and power to keep recycling them as long as necessary. His engine would be good for that much.

He studied the line of force, or whatever it was, that held him prisoner. The larger rocks within it, some of which approached his bubble in size, seemed never to change their relative positions. But smaller chunks drifted with some freedom backward and forward, at very low velocities.

He got up from his chair and turned. A single step to the rear brought him to the curve of glass. He looked out, trying to spot his enemy. Sure enough, following half a mile behind him, caught in the same string of space debris, was the berserker-ship whose pursuit had driven him here. Its scanners would be fixed on his bubble now, and it would see him moving and know he was alive. If it could get at him, it would do so. The berserker-computers would waste no time in awed contemplation of the scenery, that much was certain.

As if to register agreement with his thought, the flare of a beam weapon struck out from the berserker-ship. But the beam looked odd and silvery, and it plowed only a few yards among exploding rocks and dust before fizzling away like a comic firework. It added dust to a cloud that seemed to be thickening in front of the berserker. Probably the machine had been firing at him all along, but this weird space would not tolerate energy weapons. Missiles, then?

Yes, missiles. He watched the berserker launch one. The lean cylinder made one fiery dart in his direction, then disappeared. Where had it gone? Fallen in toward the hypermass? At invisible speed, if so.

As soon as he spotted the first flare of another missile, Karlsen on a hunch turned his eyes quickly downward. He saw an instant spark and puff in the next lower line of force, a tooth knocked out of the buzzsaw. The puff where the missile had struck flew ahead at insane speed, passing out of Karlsen's sight almost at once. His eyes were drawn after it, and he realized he had been watching the berserker-ship not with fear but with something like relief, as a distraction from facing . . . all this.

"Ah, God," he said aloud, looking ahead. It was a prayer, not an oath. Far beyond the slow-churning infinite horizon, monstrous dragon-head clouds were rearing up. Against the blackness of space their mother-of-pearl heads seemed to be formed by matter materializing out of nothingness to plunge toward the hypermass. Soon the dragons' necks rose over the edge of the world, wattled with rainbow purls of matter that dripped and fell with unreal-looking speed. And then appeared the dragon-bodies, clouds throbbing with blue-white lightning, suspended above the red bowels of hell.

The vast ring, in which Karlsen's thread of rocks was one component, raced like a circular sawblade toward the prominence. As they rushed in from the horizon they rose up far beyond Karlsen's level. They twisted and reared like mad horses. They must be bigger than planets, he thought, yes, bigger than a thousand Earths or Esteels. The whirling band he rode was going to be crushed between them—and then he saw that even as they passed they were still enormously distant from him on either side.

Karlsen let his eyes close. If men ever dared to pray, if they ever dared even to think of a Creator of the universe, it was only because their tiny minds had never been able to visualize a thousandth part . . . a millionth part . . . there were no words, no analogues for the mind to use in grasping such a scene.

And, he thought, what of men who believe only in themselves, or in nothing? What must it do to them to look nakedly at such odds as these?

Karlsen opened his eyes. In his belief a single human being was of more importance than any sun of whatever size. He made himself watch the scenery. He determined to master this almost superstitious awe.

But he had to brace himself again when he noticed for the first time how the stars were behaving. They were all blue-white needles, the wavefronts of their light jammed together in a stampede over this cliff of gravity. And his speed was such that he saw some stars moving slightly in parallax shifts. He could have depth perception in light-years, if his mind could stretch that far.

He stepped back to his chair, sat down and fastened himself in. He wanted to retreat within himself. He wanted to dig himself a tunnel, down into the very core of a huge planet where he could hide . . . but what were even the biggest planets? Poor lost specks, hardly bigger than this bubble.

Here, he faced no ordinary spaceman's view of infinity. Here there was a terrible *perspective*, starting with rocks an arm's length outside the glass and drawing the mind on and out, rock by rock and line by line, step by inescapable step, on and on and on—

All right. At least this was something to fight against, and fighting something was better than sitting here rotting. To begin with, a little routine. He drank some water, which tasted very good, and made himself eat a bite of food. He was going to be around for a while yet.

Now, for the little job of getting used to the scenery. He faced in the direction of his bubble's flight. Half a dozen meters ahead of him the first large rock, massive as the bodies of a dozen men, hung steadily in the orbit-line of force. With his mind he weighed this rock and measured it, and then moved his thought on to the next notable chunk, a pebble's throw further. The rocks were each smaller than his bubble and he could follow the string of them on and on, until it was swallowed in the converging pattern of forcelines that at last bent around the hypermass, defining the full terror of distance.

His mind hanging by its fingertips swayed out along the intervals of grandeur . . . like a baby monkey blinking in jungle sunlight, he thought. Like an infant climber who had been terrified by the size of trees and vines, who now saw them for the first time as a network of roads that could be mastered.

Now he dared to let his eyes grab hard at that buzzsaw rim of the next inner circle of hurtling rocks, to let his mind ride it out and away. Now he dared to watch the stars shifting with his movement, to see with the depth perception of a planet.

He had been through a lot even before falling here, and sleep overtook him. The next thing he knew loud noises were waking him up. He came full awake with a start of fear. The berserker was not helpless after all. Two of its man-sized machines were outside his glassy door, working on it. Karlsen reached automatically for his handgun. The little weapon was not going to do him much good, but he waited, holding it ready. There was nothing else to do.

Something was strange in the appearance of the deadly robots outside; they were silvered with a gleaming coating. It looked like frost except that it formed only on their forward surfaces, and streamed away from them toward the rear in little fringes and tails, like an artist's speed-lines made solid. The figures were substantial enough. Their hammer blows at his door . . . but wait. His fragile door was not being forced. The metal killers outside were tangled and slowed in the silvery webbing with which this mad rushing space had draped them. The stuff damped their laser beams, when they tried to burn their way in. It muffled the explosive they set off.

When they had tried everything they departed, push-

ing themselves from rock to rock back toward their
metal mother, wearing their white flaming surfaces like
hoods of shame in their defeat.

He yelled relieving insults after them. He thought of
opening his door and firing his pistol after them. He
wore a spacesuit, and if they could open the door of the
berserker-ship from inside he should be able to open
this one. But he decided it would be a waste of ammunition.

Some deep part of his mind had concluded that it was
better for him, in his present situation, not to think
about time. He saw no reason to argue with this decision, and so he soon lost track of hours and days—
weeks?

He exercised and shaved, he ate and drank and
eliminated. The boat's recycling systems worked very
well. He still had his "coffin," and might choose a
long sleep—but no thanks, not yet. The possibility of
rescue was in his thoughts, mixing hope with his fears
of time. He knew that on the day he fell down here there
was no ship built capable of coming after him and
pulling him out. But ships were always being im-
proved. Suppose he could hang on here for a few weeks
or months of subjective time while a few years passed
outside. He knew there were people who would try to
find him and save him if there was any hope.

From being almost paralyzed by his surroundings, he
passed through a stage of exaltation, and then quickly
reached—boredom. The mind had its own business,
and turned itself away from all these eternal blazing
miracles. He slept a good deal.

In a dream he saw himself standing alone in space.

He was viewing himself at the distance where the human figure dwindles almost to a speck in the gaze of the unaided human eye. With an almost invisible arm, himself-in-the-distance waved good-bye, and then went walking away, headed out toward the blue-white stars. The striding leg movements were at first barely perceptible, and then became nothing at all as the figure dwindled, losing existence against the face of the deep. . . .

With a yell he woke up. A space boat had nudged against his crystal hull, and was now bobbing a few feet away. It was a solid metal ovoid, of a model he recognized, and the numbers and letters on its hull were familiar to him. He had made it. He had hung on. The ordeal was over.

The little hatch of the rescue boat opened, and two suited figures emerged, one after the other, from its sheltered interior. At once these figures became silver-blurred as the berserker's machines had been, but these men's features were visible through their faceplates, their eyes looking straight at Karlsen. They smiled in steady encouragement, never taking their eyes from his.

Not for an instant.

They rapped on his door, and kept smiling while he put on his spacesuit. But he made no move to let them in; instead he drew his gun.

They frowned. Inside their helmets their mouths formed words: Open up! He flipped on his radio, but if they were sending nothing was coming through in this space. They kept on gazing steadily at him.

Wait, he signaled with an upraised hand. He got a slate and stylus from his chair, and wrote them a message.

LOOK AROUND AT THE SCENERY FOR A WHILE.

He was sane but maybe they thought him mad. As if to humor him, they began to look around them. A new set of dragon-head prominences were rising ahead, beyond the stormy horizon at the rim of the world. The frowning men looked ahead of them at dragons, around them at buzzsaw rainbow whirls of stone, they looked down into the deadly depths of the inferno, they looked up at the stars' poisonous blue-white spears sliding visibly over the void.

Then both of them, still frowning uncomprehendingly, looked right back at Karlsen.

He sat in his chair, holding his drawn gun, waiting, having no more to say. He knew the berserker-ship would have boats aboard, and that it could build its killing machines into the likenesses of men. These were almost good enough to fool him.

The figures outside produced a slate of their own from somewhere.

WE TOOK BERS. FROM BEHIND. ALL OK & SAFE. COME OUT.

He looked back. The cloud of dust raised by the berserker's own weapons had settled around it, hiding it and all the forceline behind it from Karlsen's view. Oh, if only he could believe that these were men . . .

They gestured energetically, and lettered some more.

OUR SHIP WAITING BACK THERE BEHIND

241

DUST. SHE'S TOO BIG TO HOLD THIS LEVEL LONG.

And again:

KARLSEN, COME WITH US! ! ! THIS YOUR ONLY CHANCE!

He didn't dare read any more of their messages for fear he would believe them, rush out into their metal arms, and be torn apart. He closed his eyes and prayed. After a long time he opened his eyes again. His visitors and their boats were gone.

Not long afterward—as time seemed to him—there were flashes of light from inside the dust cloud surrounding the berserker. A fight, to which someone had brought weapons that would work in this space? Or another attempt to trick him? He would see.

He was watching alertly as another rescue boat, much like the first, inched its way out of the dustcloud toward him. It drew alongside and stopped. Two more spacesuited figures got out and began to wear silver drapery.

This time he had his sign ready.

LOOK AROUND AT THE SCENERY FOR A WHILE.

As if to humor him, they began to look around them. Maybe they thought him mad, but he was sane. After about a minute they still hadn't turned back to him— one's face looked up and out at the unbelievable stars, while the other slowly swiveled his neck, watching a dragon's head go by. Gradually their bodies became congealed in awe and terror, clinging and crouching against his glass wall.

After taking half a minute more to check his own

helmet and suit, Karlsen bled out his cabin air and opened his door.

"Welcome, *men*," he said, over his helmet radio. He had to help one of them aboard the rescue boat. But they made it.

BEST-SELLING
Science Fiction
and
Fantasy

MORE SCIENCE FICTION! ADVENTURE

THE CHILDE CYCLE SERIES

By Gordon R. Dickson

Available at your local bookstore or return this form to: